TILL THE DAY I DIE

Shot at point-blank range while trying to prevent the kidnapping of her daughter Becky, book editor Catherine Desmond has a mysterious near-death experience. When she recovers, she learns that Becky has been murdered by a gang of child abusers, who are still active and being hunted by the police. To her dismay, she finds herself linked psychically with Becky's killer — and he begins shadowing her as well. An ethereal cat-and-mouse game ensues, with life — and death — hanging in the balance . . .

Books by V. J. Banis
in the Linford Mystery Library:

THE WOLVES OF CRAYWOOD
THE GLASS PAINTING
WHITE JADE
DARKWATER
I AM ISABELLA
THE GLASS HOUSE
MOON GARDEN
THE SECOND HOUSE
ROSE POINT
THE DEVIL'S DANCE
SHADOWS
HOUSE OF FOOLS
FIVE GREEN MEN
THE SCENT OF HEATHER
THE BISHOP'S PALACE
BLOOD MOON
FIRE ON THE MOON
FATAL FLOWERS
THE LION'S GATE

V. J. BANIS

TILL THE DAY I DIE

Complete and Unabridged

LINFORD
Leicester

First published in Great Britain

First Linford Edition
published 2016

A catalogue record for this book is available
from the British Library.

ISBN 978–1–4448–2734–7

Published by
F. A. Thorpe (Publishing)
Anstey, Leicestershire

Set by Words & Graphics Ltd.
Anstey, Leicestershire
Printed and bound in Great Britain by
T. J. International Ltd., Padstow, Cornwall

This book is printed on acid-free paper

1

It was just as she'd always heard it described: the tunnel, the blinding white light, and everyone waiting to greet her — gosh, that was her father, wasn't it, and there was . . .

'Catherine.' She heard her name distinctly, from somewhere behind. She looked back, and saw Jack in the distance. Jack? That wasn't possible, surely, not after all these years?

'Catherine,' he called again, 'Come back. You can't go yet.'

Ahead, her loved ones waited for her. When she tried to look at them, however, actually to see them, there were no images. It was more as if she felt them. She simply knew they were there, and she wanted to join them, truly she did. She couldn't go back.

And yet . . . someone — *some thing* — separated itself from the light; something of light itself, but so bright, so intense, that she could not bear to look directly at it.

'You must go back.' It was like a voice inside her head. 'You must find him. There is something that you must do, that only you can do.'

'I can't go back. Please, it's more than I could bear.'

But it was too late. Already she could feel herself returning, the voices fading, the light retreating, further and further . . .

Until she heard a triumphant voice say, 'We've got her. She's alive.'

★ ★ ★

'Can you hear me?'

Catherine forced her eyes open. A white-jacketed man leaned over her. She was in a hospital bed. She tried to move her hand, to wipe away the fog, but the hand wouldn't move. Her legs . . .

'Don't try to talk, not yet,' the doctor said. 'You've had a narrow escape.'

Someone said, 'We have to ask her some questions.'

'Not now.' The doctor's voice was firm.

There were two strangers behind the doctor, a dark-suited man and a woman with frizzy orange hair. Beyond them, Walter, her husband, watched with red-rimmed eyes. Seeing him, she remembered: the parking lot, her daughter, the yellow-bearded man. She managed to croak one word: 'Becky?'

Walter began to cry, tears streaming down his cheeks. 'She's dead, Cathy,' he sobbed aloud. 'The police found her body. Becky's dead.'

* * *

The scene kept playing over and over in her mind. She came out of the market and saw the empty Buick where Walter and Becky should have been waiting, one door wide open. Her eyes raked the crowded parking lot and she saw them, Becky and the two men trying to force her into a rusty black pick-up. 'Mommy, Mommy, help me!' Becky cried.

'Becky! Stop, let her go!' Catherine dropped the bags of groceries and ran toward the little girl struggling in the arms of two men.

One of them clambered into the truck, dragging Becky with him. The other — tall, skinny — shoved her toward the middle of the seat and tried to get in after her.

Catherine caught the door. 'No,' she screamed, 'I won't let you!'

He swore and tried to kick her away with one foot in the belly. She gagged with the pain, but her hands still held on to the door.

'Get away, bitch!' He bared his teeth and yanked the glove box open, pulling out a gun.

'Mommy!' Becky sobbed loudly. The truck's engine roared to life.

Somewhere behind her, Catherine heard Walter cry, 'Catherine! Becky!' but she wouldn't take her eyes from the man with the gun.

'Give me back my daughter!' The truck began to move. 'Give her back!'

He held the gun practically in her face, and fired. Her fingers slipped from the flailing truck door. Gears ground, tires squealed. Her head hit the pavement and blackness fell over her.

★   ★   ★

'It's my fault,' Walter said, voice breaking. 'It was only a couple of minutes, I swear it. We walked over to look in the window, at the toy store, you know, and I had just put Becky back in the car when this man came up and said I had dropped my wallet.

' 'Back there,' he said, 'back by the toy store,' so I walked back to look for it, but I couldn't find it. Then I heard you scream, and I saw . . . ' He choked back a sob.

She would have to forgive him. Someday. She understood what guilt he was suffering. For now, though, her grief was all she could manage.

★   ★   ★

She had hardly any more to say to the investigators who came the next day to see her: L.A.P.D. Sergeant Jess Conners,

5

and a woman with frizzy orange hair who introduced herself as Agent Chang with the Federal Bureau of Investigation. 'Child Abduction and Serial Killers Unit,' she added. 'CASKU. Most of the guys just call me Chang.' She hesitated briefly. 'We're sorry to trouble you now. But in these cases the sooner we can gather information the better our chances are of resolving them.'

'*Cases?*'

'We think these men have done this before.'

Catherine wanted to help, truly. She gave them what she could. 'It was an old truck, black, rusty. A GMC, I think. I didn't see the license.'

'Can you describe the men for me? There were two of them?'

'Yes. One burly — I barely got a glimpse of his face; he was big, that's all I know, like a bear. The one nearest me, he was tall and skinny. A mole on his chin. Crooked nose.'

'Like it had been broken?'

'Yes. Green eyes. Yellow beard, unkempt. Not blond, yellow. Like it had been dyed.'

'Don't worry, Mrs. Desmond, we'll find them. We'll get these monsters, I promise you.'

'You've got to go now,' the little Filipina nurse, Millie, told the federal agent. 'She has to rest.'

Catherine was grateful for Millie, as grateful as she could be now for anything. Millie understood; she asked no questions, offered no well-meaning condolences. She simply did everything she could to ease Catherine's discomfort.

★　★　★

'This will seem a little strange to you.' The doctor was one Catherine hadn't seen before, a pale blonde woman. The light from the window formed a golden halo about her head. They had finally removed the last of Catherine's bandages, leaving her scalp feeling oddly naked.

The doctor raised a small penlight in front of Catherine's face and flicked it on. Intense light filled Catherine's vision. It reminded her of that other light, blinding, pure. It began to seem to her that she could see something in *this* light — almost see something, if she just looked a little harder.

She was only vaguely aware of what the doctor was saying: 'You must travel. You must learn it. Try, just a little way. I will help.'

Suddenly, Catherine was in the corridor outside, and Millie was coming along the hallway. Millie looked up and saw her and blinked, disbelieving.

As suddenly as she had left it, Catherine was back in her bed, pain threatening to make her head explode. She had forgotten the doctor tending her until she said, 'Hurts, doesn't it?'

Catherine opened her eyes. The door flew open and Millie dashed into the room. The doctor did not even seem to notice the sudden entrance.

'You're here,' Millie said. 'I thought . . . '

The doctor smiled. 'How could she go anywhere?' she asked.

Millie shook her head. 'How silly of me. How could you go anywhere?' She backed out of the room, her puzzled eyes studying Catherine's face.

Catherine looked at the doctor. 'Why did you say that?' she asked.

'Say what?'

'That; what you said . . . about traveling?'

The woman chuckled. 'My dear, I'm afraid it will be a while before you do any real traveling. You rest now.' She strolled toward the door.

'Wait,' Catherine said, 'I — I'm confused.'

At the door, the doctor paused for just a second to look back and smile. 'Of course you are. It will get better, I promise. It just takes time.'

★ ★ ★

It felt strange to be back in Los Angeles. Jack McKenzie took the freeway ramp for Hollywood Boulevard. The volume of traffic had doubled in the dozen or so years since he had been here.

One thing that blessedly hadn't changed was Musso and Frank's. The restaurant sat where it had sat for ages, defending its faded elegance against the growing

9

seediness of Hollywood Boulevard. He left his car in the parking lot in the rear, slipping the attendant a ten to insure that he kept an eye on it, and entered by the back door and the little corridor that went past the kitchen.

It brought him to a room with a monumental mahogany bar, with faded and vaguely pastoral murals and high-backed wooden booths where generations of stars, politicians and moguls had sipped their cocktails and eaten the unchanged list of daily specials.

Peter Weitman was already in one of the booths, sipping a martini. A second one waited in its little bowl of ice for Jack. In the years since they had last met, Weitman had added some extra pounds to his never-trim build and traded much of his hair for them, but the eyes in the round face looked up at Jack with undiminished shrewdness.

'I hope your tastes haven't changed,' he said, indicating the waiting martini as Jack slipped into the booth across from him.

'Not that much.' They shook hands

quickly. By that time, a waiter had appeared to pour Jack's drink into the chilled stemmed glass. Jack nodded his thanks and took a sip. 'Ah. Nobody does it better, I swear.'

Peter lifted his glass. 'Welcome back to La-La Land.' He had a sip of his own drink. 'How does it feel?'

'A little funny. For all its tackiness, it does have a charm of its own.'

'Admittedly a wacky charm,' Peter agreed. He hesitated and looked down at his martini. 'Did you hear about Catherine?'

'I heard that she married Walter. That was years ago. I don't suppose you're going to tell me they're divorced.'

'Her daughter was killed. Kidnapped.'

'Jesus!' Jack slammed his drink down so hard that the stem on the glass broke. In an instant, a waiter was there.

They sat in silence until the waiter brought a new glass with a fresh drink. He set it down and gave Peter and the menus a meaningful glance. Peter shook his head and the waiter disappeared again.

'God, she must be crazy with grief,' Jack said finally.

'She was nearly killed herself.' Peter told him the whole story, so far as he knew it. Jack listened without interruption. He was thinking, if only he could have been there to comfort her. Of course, she didn't love him; she was married to another man — had married him within weeks of the day he had left Los Angeles — so whatever love she felt for Walter must have been there all along.

Peter finished his story and waited for Jack to respond. The silence grew uncomfortably long. He was about to speak up himself when at last Jack looked directly at him for the first time in many minutes.

'Let's talk about that job you mentioned,' he said.

⋆ ⋆ ⋆

It was nearly a month before she could go home. Brain damage, stroke danger, seizures, black-outs — none of which mattered to her in the least. If she couldn't die, couldn't trade places with her daughter, what did it matter how she lived?

She never saw the woman doctor again, the one who had spoken to her of traveling. No one seemed to know who she was.

'There are so many doctors here,' Nurse Millie said when Catherine questioned her. 'It's hard to keep track of them all.' Millie was different now; the easy intimacy that had existed between them before had vanished. She was wary with Catherine, uncomfortable in Catherine's presence.

★　★　★

Her mother was at the house when they got there. 'I won't be in the way,' Sandra Dodd promised, wary, because up till now when she had visited at the hospital, her daughter had been distant and uncommunicative. 'I'll just finish getting dinner ready and then I'll go home.'

'Maybe you should stay for a night or two,' Walter said. 'I'll have to go to work.'

'I'll be all right,' Catherine said, and,

more emphatically, 'Really.'

She glanced around at the living room, at a vase filled with yellow roses that sat atop the piano. 'Thank you for the flowers, Mom.'

'Oh, they're not . . . ' Sandra hesitated. Part of her wanted to let the mistake stand, but she couldn't. 'They aren't from me.' Catherine raised a questioning eyebrow. 'They're from Jack. Jack McKenzie.'

'McKenzie?' Walter said. 'I didn't even know he was back in town, did you?' The look he gave Catherine was accusing.

'I've rather been out of circulation.' She took the note from the roses and read it.

'What the hell does he want?'

She handed him the note. It was simple to the point of austerity: 'My sincere sympathy. Jack McKenzie.'

Jack McKenzie. As if he needed to add his last name. As if she might have forgotten who he was. But she didn't want to think of Jack; *wouldn't* think of him. That, surely, was the feather that would tip her over the edge into the bottomless pit if anything would.

Walter took the card and read it for a long moment as though the message it contained was a lengthy one. 'Have you seen him?' he asked finally.

She sighed. 'I haven't spoken to Jack since he left thirteen years ago.'

He crumpled up the card and threw it violently into the wastebasket by the desk.

'Did I hear a baaing sound?' Sandra asked. 'I do believe there's a lamb stew calling for my attention.' She left the room to give them tactful space for anything that needed saying. There was, she thought, quite a bit of that, none of which she needed to hear.

Whatever that might have been, however, remained unsaid in a silence that eddied around husband and wife. Catherine went to the bay window and stared out at the back garden. The flowers were wilted, the grass brown from lack of water. The leaves of the maple tree hung down dispiritedly.

'I'd better get to the restaurant,' Walter said. 'If you have any ... If you need anything, call me on my cell.'

15

'I'll be all right,' she said again. Relenting, if only slightly, she came to give him a perfunctory kiss.

When he had gone; when she heard the car door slam, heard the Buick pull out of the driveway and move off down the street; when she was sure he wasn't coming back but was truly on his way to the restaurant he owned in Santa Monica, she went to the wastebasket and retrieved the card, smoothing it out.

They had been rivals, Walter and Jack, if unequal ones. It had always been Jack who had ruled in her heart, though she liked Walter well enough, and felt kindly toward him.

'You're sweet. I do like you, honestly,' was the best she could give him then; and that, of course, was not enough for a man in love. *What can I do?* she asked herself. She couldn't help being in love with Jack any more than Walter could help being in love with her.

I mustn't think of this, she told herself severely. *I mustn't remember.* From the kitchen she heard the rattle of cups and silverware as her mother set the table. She started to throw the card away again, but instead she dropped it into the pocket of her denim skirt.

2

The house stifled her. Everywhere she looked she found memories of Becky. She tried to watch television, and instead of Oprah, she found herself watching Becky's one-time favorite show, *Daffy Danny's Alley*. It was a passion that Becky had shared with a great many pre-teens, and one that (thankfully, so far as Catherine was concerned) she had quickly outgrown. Catherine had come into the den one day to discover Becky watching cartoons instead.

'No *Daffy Danny*?' she had asked.

Becky's answer was brief and to the point: 'He's smarmy.'

An opinion Catherine shared. 'Danny' was Danny O'Dell, host and hand-puppeteer, an altogether too-fey young man — or, probably not really so young, but who worked hard at that illusion — who wore too-short trousers and a too-tight checked jacket and a tam with a red pom-pom, and who mugged a little too outrageously for the benefit of the squealing girls in the studio audience. In the past she had gritted her teeth while Becky sat enrapt, from 'Kids, what time is it? It's *Daffy Danny* time,' through every 'daffy laffy,' to the last 'daffy bye bye,' delivered with a big kiss thrown at the television screen.

Now, of course, she would have kissed Danny O'Dell herself if it could have brought her daughter back to her.

* * *

She went back to work finally at Dean and Summers, Publishers, both glad to have her time occupied and sorry to have to face the well-meant expressions of sympathy when people saw her.

'Catherine,' Fermin Dean greeted her with evident delight. He was tall and gaunt, silver-haired, one of those people who seem to be in motion even when sitting still. He bounded up from his chair and came round his desk to clasp her hands. 'It's good to have you back.'

'I'll be glad for the work. I can use the occupation,' she said.

'Don't overdo it. And I mean this, Catherine — make your own hours, please.'

Even with his warning, she was not quite prepared for the workload waiting for her, despite everyone's obvious efforts to keep things moving along. Books that ought to have been in production by now had been held up for months, and newer projects waited for her green light. A mountain of correspondence, most of it submissions for book proposals, filled up half of her desk and overflowed onto a chair.

She threw herself into her work, the best antidote she had found yet for the pain. Not that the pain ever quite went away. It merely curled itself up into a little knot in a far corner of her mind, where it ever waited to come back out into the light.

Her assistant, Bill — black and gay — worked closely with her each day, but she had learned early on that he was a very model of discretion, a fact for which she could be grateful now.

★ ★ ★

At first, Catherine went every day after work to Forest Lawn Memorial Park, to bring flowers to Becky's grave. She and Becky used to come here in the past, not as morbid a destination as one might have supposed. There were fountains and gardens, and an uncanny look-alike of Michelangelo's David.

The winter rains came. They did not deter her, though by now she went only once or twice a week. The gravesite was on a knoll from which bright green lawns, salt-and-peppered with gravesites, spilled down to the Golden State Freeway with its endless rush of cars.

At home, she and Walter shared the house; they moved about in the same finite space; and yet they remained light-years apart. Sometimes she could hear him in his office, crying. Most of the time he watched her warily with red-rimmed eyes and sniffled until she thought she must scream; but how could she, eyes tearless, rail at him for his grief?

He spent more and more time at the restaurant. She had no doubt that he found it more comfortable away from her, just as she was relieved to see him go. It was not that she hated him, or that she even consciously blamed him for what had happened. They could hardly share their home day by day, however, without reminding one another of what was missing from it.

He had lost ten pounds and gained ten years. He looked faded, too, like a shirt too often washed. It wasn't only Becky those two men had killed, she thought grimly. They were killing Catherine and Walter Desmond day by day.

A casual question one day — 'Will your mother be coming for Christmas?' — made her aware of the time she hadn't noticed passing.

The question caught her by surprise. 'Is it December?'

'The second.'

Which meant, she realized, that Thanksgiving had come and gone without her noticing. They had always made such a big deal of it in the past. Becky had been quite set in her preferences. The turkey's wings were hers, both of them, and woe betide the foolish mortal who thought to claim one. The pie must be pumpkin.

'I hadn't thought that far ahead,' she told Walter. She got up and began to clear the table, but she did manage to rest a hand, briefly, on his shoulder. She really did wish she could comfort him.

A fire-engine-red Bronco pulled into the driveway shortly after he had gone. At first she didn't recognize the woman who got out and walked briskly to the door. Not until she had rung the bell and Catherine had studied her long and hard through the glass in the front door did she realize that it was the FBI agent who had interviewed her in the hospital. 'Agent Chang,' she greeted her, ushering her inside.

'Just Chang. Or you can call me Roby, if you like. As in Roberta.' She saw the familiar puzzlement and waited for the customary question.

'You must get told a lot that that doesn't sound Chinese.'

'Not as much as I hear, 'Funny, you don't look Jewish.' Daddy's the Chinese part. Momma was a Jewish princess. Still is, to tell the truth, but she would have a

23

fit if she heard me say it. That explains this, too.' She put a hand up to her spiky orange hair. 'I'm afraid I'm the classic American mongrel.'

'Maybe hybrid is the better word,' Catherine said. 'Come in, please. Can I get you something? Coffee? A drink?'

'Nothing, thanks, I won't stay long.' She looked around, avoiding Catherine's eyes.

'Have you come with news? Have you found them?' Hope flared for a moment.

Chang looked directly at her then and Catherine knew the answer before the agent shook her head. 'Nothing, unfortunately. Actually, I was hoping you might have something for me. I thought maybe you had remembered something after all this time, some detail that you forgot earlier.'

Catherine hated having to disappoint her. 'Nothing that I didn't tell you before.'

'There's been another one. Several, actually, over the last few months, but a couple of them look awfully similar to your . . . your case. Yesterday a girl got snatched from a shopping mall. The mother got just a glimpse, but the description she gave us sounded like the same two men.'

'That poor woman.' Catherine swallowed a lump that rose in her throat and looked away. 'There's something that I've ... I've struggled for hours at a time to understand: how anyone could do what these men do. Can you help me to understand that, Agent Chang?'

Roby Chang sighed deeply. She had struggled with that same question many times, and every answer she came up with ultimately seemed inadequate.

'I think it's the innocence of their victims,' she said. 'These animals — I won't call them men, they aren't that — they see that innocence, what we perceive of as something beautiful and precious, and to them it appears as a stain, as a flaw in their scheme of things, and they feel compelled to remove that stain.' Like all the others, this answer too sounded inadequate when she tried to put it into words. 'There's more to it than that, of course. Money.'

'But, they never asked for ransom. There wasn't time for that.'

Crapola, Chang thought silently. She took a deep breath. 'Often they take pictures, films. There is a big market for that sick sort of thing. Kiddie porn, it's called.'

Catherine turned away from her and leaned against the window frame, head bent. After a moment, she asked in a breaking voice, 'Are you telling me that somewhere there are pictures, movies, floating around that show . . . that show my Becky being violated?'

'There may well be. What I don't get is, why did they . . . ?' For a moment she had gone into agent-mode, thinking aloud. 'I'm sorry.'

'No. Go on, please. What is it that you don't get?'

'Well, like I said, there's movies and pictures. They're worth a lot of money. And then, after that, usually they . . . you know, they pass them on.'

'For sex, you mean?'

'Yes.' Chang was clearly embarrassed with the information she was imparting to

Catherine's back. Should she go on, or try to soft-pedal it? Yet her instinct was that this woman truly wanted — *needed* — to know. 'The point is, these children are worth far more to them alive than dead.'

'Then why . . . ?'

'If I knew that . . . ' Chang shrugged again.

Catherine was quiet for so long that Chang wondered if perhaps she should simply leave. When Catherine finally did speak, it was to say, her voice cracking, 'I tried to protect her. I tried to shield her from the evil of the world.'

Chang had seen this same bewildered grief in other parents who had lost a child to murder. She had seen marriages, families torn apart by such guilt. Even when justice was served, even when memory faded, no parent of a murdered child ever afterward swam blissfully in the river of forgetfulness.

She took a card from her wallet and handed it to Catherine. 'Meantime, if you think of anything . . . sometimes memory does funny things, you know; the most trivial thing will trigger something in your mind. If you think of anything, anything at all, call me. Day or night.'

★ ★ ★

Since her return from the hospital, Catherine had been sleeping in Becky's room. That night she returned to her own bed, to Walter.

He welcomed her into his arms, and after several long moments of silent embrace, he tried dutifully to make love to her. At length, he heaved a deep sigh and rolled off of her.

'I'm sorry,' he said.

For a reply, she took his hand and gave it a forgiving squeeze. Later, when he began to snore gently in his sleep, she went back to Becky's room.

Lying there in the darkness, the futility of their attempt at sex stayed with her. Yet now that she was in another bed, another room; now that she considered it at a safe distance, she realized that nothing sexual had happened between them for a long while, even before.

She had not minded; had welcomed the absence, she supposed; had scarcely even been conscious of it. If she had been able to see the future, she might well have considered another child ... but who could possibly have foreseen what happened?

She got up and went into the bathroom — not the master bath, which was too close to where he slept, but the one across the hall from Becky's room. The door closed, all the lights on, she shed her robe and took a long, hard look at herself in the mirror.

She had never been beautiful, not even as a young woman, but she had known without conceit that she was attractive to the opposite sex. That, however, had been years ago. Was she still? She honestly didn't know. Walter didn't count. She had not for many years thought of him in terms of sex, opposite or otherwise. And, it seemed, the same with him.

She had a good complexion and eyes the color of old cognac. She was thirty-two. Well-preserved, she thought with all due modesty. Until this last year, she had

29

been careful of diet and exercise. When she got on the scales, she saw that she had gained a full five pounds. Too much time abed, not enough exercise.

Even so, she didn't exactly look chubby. Would a man still find her attractive? Would — *the time for pretense in your life is past, my girl,* she told herself — would Jack McKenzie still find her attractive?

Memories crowded in upon her, sweet, stinging. She had been seventeen when they had met. Eighteen when they first made love — the night of her eighteenth birthday, to be exact. His scruples, not hers. Despite her most ardent efforts to convince him otherwise, he had stubbornly insisted that he wanted her to be an adult when it happened. 'I'm not robbing any cradles, my love,' he insisted. He was eight years older than she. Eight years wiser, she could see now, though at the time she had seen it only as sheer pigheadedness. Pigheadedness that somehow allowed her to convince herself that he didn't love her when he said they would have to wait to get married.

'Why do you have to go away, to the Middle East?' she demanded.

'Because I plan to be a war correspondent.' He had been so calm, so reasonable, that it only enraged her all the more. 'Iraq is where the war is going to be. Iraq, Kuwait, Saudi Arabia — that's where I have to be.'

'Then I'll go with you.'

The tolerant smile he gave her infuriated her. 'There's no way I would take you there. No, my darling, you will wait here until I come back. Assuming I do come back. There's always that chance.'

'And if I won't wait?'

'Kat, don't be silly. If it will make you feel better, we'll get married the first day I step on US soil again, I promise.'

'Why don't we get married now, and you go do your Mideast thing, and I will wait here for you. We have a week for a honeymoon, surely, before you have to leave.'

There was that damned smile again. 'Suppose I didn't come back? Suppose I left you pregnant? What family do you have? Your mother, who is caring for a bedridden husband at the present? And I have a cousin in Oregon, who probably barely remembers me. No — you're young, you're single; I want you to enjoy your life, have fun. You're still a kid. Go out with other guys if you feel like it. There'll be plenty of time to work on marriage when I get back.'

He went, and she sent his ring to him without even a note, and before six months had passed she married Walter. What a fool she had been.

The shooting had left an ugly scar at her left temple. She tugged her hair down over it, pulling and fluffing until she had managed to hide it from sight. After a moment, she made a grimace of regret at herself and gathering her robe from the floor, tossed it about her shoulders. Before she turned the light out, she gave the image in the mirror one last glance.

She could not help wondering: how would Jack McKenzie see her now?

★ ★ ★

It seemed to Catherine that she had barely closed her eyes when a voice said, 'Wake up.'

She opened her eyes, but the white light that filled the room blinded her and she could see nothing.

'You must come,' the voice said. 'Come see.'

The light faded and she was standing in an unfamiliar room, a seedy room with faded wallpaper hanging loose from the ceiling and dust motes dancing in the pale light. There were two men on a bed — and a little girl with them.

On cue, the girl cried out with a sob, 'Don't, don't, please.'

A giant bear of a man, his back to Catherine, chuckled. The other one — long, skinny — said, 'Shut up, or I'll tape your mouth again.'

Catherine tried to scream, to call out to them to leave the girl alone, but no sound came. She took a step toward the bed. She must make them stop. This was too horrible to bear.

Despite her silence, perhaps because he sensed her presence, the skinny man raised his head and looked in her direction, looked directly at her. Her heart thudded. It was him: the man with the yellow beard. The beard was gone now, shaved off, making his face look different, but she would never forget those eyes; nothing could disguise that face from her.

'What the hell?' he said. He jumped up from the bed and took a step in her direction. The other man looked too; she had a quick glimpse of his face as he said, 'Trash can?'

The next instant she was back in bed in Becky's room, lightning shards of pain crashing through her head.

She barely reached the toilet bowl in time to vomit wildly into it. Even when her stomach was emptied the dry heaves continued for long minutes.

Finally, weakly, she sat on the edge of the bathtub. As her head began to clear, she thought of Agent Chang. She ran to the den where she had left the F.B.I. agent's card and was actually dialing the number before she thought to wonder what she was going to tell her. That she had seen her daughter's kidnappers in a dream? With another little girl, perhaps the very one who had disappeared yesterday?

She returned the receiver to its cradle. Chang would think she was insane. *Maybe I am*, she thought. How could she explain what had just happened? Who would believe her?

Had it been only a dream? She had seen Yellow Beard jump up from the bed, and heard him exclaim. Heard the other man on the bed say, 'trash can.' Which made no sense.

Dreams didn't, though, did they?

3

She woke with the memory of that horrible nightmare still fresh in her mind. She wished she could share her experience with someone, and at once dismissed her husband. He would shrug it off as hysteria and grief.

Her mother? As if that thought had communicated itself through space, the phone rang and it was her mother. 'I have to do some shopping,' Sandra Dodd said, her tone making a question of it, 'and I thought you might join me? We could have lunch together.'

Shopping and lunch had been a monthly ritual in the past, one of the many that had fallen by the wayside. 'Dominique's, in the mall?' Catherine suggested.

'At twelve?' Sandra was obviously delighted.

After she had hung up the phone, however, Catherine was less sure. The thought of the mall crowds, the early

Christmas crowds especially, intimidated her. She felt the urge to stay in her safe retreat, where no one could assault her.

Only, they had assaulted her, if only in her dreams. Staying in was no safer than going out, if her mind wasn't free. By the time she was dressed to go out, her mood was decidedly cheerless.

★　★　★

The mall parking lot was crowded and she had to drive around for several minutes before she finally found a space. Even so, she was early. She sat for a brief while, listening to the sound of rain on the car roof and trying to screw up the courage to go inside.

Dominique, the restaurant's petite and pretty proprietress, was happy to see her. 'Mrs. Desmond, how delightful,' she greeted her. 'We've missed you.'

Which meant, Catherine imagined, that she did not know the reason for the absence. She ordered a glass of Chablis and told the waitress she would wait for her mother to join her.

When the wine came, she took a sip without tasting it. She looked about her at the other diners, a decidedly mixed lot: more women than men, lots of children, a few teenagers. In the background, Bing Crosby dreamed faintly of a white Christmas. At the table next to hers, a young boy, eight or perhaps nine, got up from the table and told his mother he was going to the restroom.

'Give me a minute,' she sighed. She emptied her coffee cup and started to collect her packages.

'No, I want to go alone,' he said firmly.

It was a youngster's predictable push for adolescent independence and after a moment's consideration, the mother nodded. 'Straight there and straight back,' she said, and motioned to the waitress for more coffee.

Catherine watched the boy stride away, shoulders proud and straight, and felt a sudden wave of fear, of horrible expectation. He looked so very young, so vulnerable with his thin wrists showing out the cuffs of a shirt he had nearly outgrown. She thought of the brief time in which Becky had been taken.

Without thinking of what she was doing or how she might appear, she leaped up so suddenly that she startled the approaching waitress.

'Please.' She stepped to the woman's table. 'Please, you mustn't let him go alone. It isn't safe.'

The woman looked up at her in surprise and suspicion. She glanced at the waitress as if to say, who let this fruitcake in? 'What's not safe? The mall? For Pete's sake, there's a million people here today. I think you should mind your own business.'

'Ma'am.' The waitress tried to intervene.

'I'm sorry, I . . . ' Catherine realized suddenly how she must look. Probably they thought she was mad. She backed away in confusion, snatching up her purse, the umbrella forgotten altogether, and dashed out of the restaurant. 'Tell my mother something has come up,' she told a startled Dominique. 'Tell her . . . she'll understand.'

She ran through the corridors of the

mall, ignoring the puzzled looks of the shoppers she jostled and sidestepped, ran through the glass doors to the parking lot — and ran into Jack McKenzie.

Ran into him, literally. Head down, she plunged through the glass doors, already fumbling in her purse for the car keys — and collided with someone.

Hands caught her arms to steady her and an astonished voice said, 'Catherine? My God, it's you.'

She stepped back, looked up — and felt her heart stop inside her. 'Jack?' She could not believe this could possibly be happening.

'Have I gone downhill that badly?' he asked, making a joke to hide his own confusion. She looked wild-eyed, frantic. God, what more could have happened to her? He held himself in check by a sheer effort of will.

'No.' She shook her head emphatically. 'You look ... ' She was going to say 'wonderful,' but amended it to ' ... good. I just ... I wasn't expecting to see you.'

'Well, no, of course you wouldn't be. Me neither.' He glanced around and up and seemed to realize for the first time that they were standing in the rain. 'Look, maybe we should step inside.'

He held tightly to her arm and pulled the door open with his other hand to lead her inside. They paused by the skating rink. It seemed as if neither of them could think of anything to say. He realized belatedly that he was still holding on to her and let his hand drop. 'How are you?' was the best he could manage.

'I'm all right,' she said hoarsely. 'Thank you for the roses.'

He shook his head. 'Catherine, I felt so awful for you. I wanted . . . I wanted to come to you, but I didn't think . . . '

She managed a lopsided smile. 'No, it's best that you didn't. Walter . . . ' She left it at that. She lifted a hand unconsciously to tug a damp curl over the scar at her temple, and as she did, the sparkle of her wedding ring caught his eye.

'Yes,' he said, the shards of light seeming to pierce his heart. He took the gesture for deliberate. 'Walter.'

The silence now was awkward. He took a step back from her. 'Well,' he said again.

'Are you . . . ?' She wanted to ask, *Are you married, are you in love?* Instead, she asked, 'Back to stay?'

'For a while, at least. Peter gave me a job at the station. Peter Weitman, you remember him? Channel three at four. I reveal my ignorance on the state of the world.'

She looked long and hard at him. He had changed, of course he had. The truth was, she thought the changes were for the better. The hair was close-cut now, and there was a dusting of gray at the temples, which gave him an air of distinction. The gray-blue eyes studying her were still as piercing as ever.

'Catherine,' he blurted out, too painfully aware of her expression of embarrassment (was it that awkward for her, just seeing him?), 'I'm sorry about everything in the past. But that's what it is, the past. Surely now we could be friends.'

Which, she thought, settled that nicely and put her squarely in her place, in case she might entertain any ideas of something more.

'I don't see why we shouldn't.' She

made her voice business-like. 'I've got to go. It was good seeing you. Welcome back.'

Just like that, she was gone. He stood and stared after her, watched her dash across the parking lot, saw her climb into her car, waited until it had disappeared into the rain.

And what had he expected, anyway? That after all these years she would throw herself into his arms; would tell him that she did after all love him; that nothing mattered any more but them, together at last?

★   ★   ★

At home, Catherine stripped off her sodden clothes and slipped into a robe. The telephone rang but she ignored it. A fire was already laid in the living room fireplace, and she lit it and poured herself a glass of cognac.

She didn't often drink these days, afraid that she would find that too convenient a relief. Now, though, the burn of the alcohol in her throat was welcome.

She was still unnerved by the meeting with Jack. Seeing him, however briefly, however disappointingly, was like stepping from an icy cold outside into a warm, firelit room. She could almost feel the frigidity within her begin to thaw, like the heat from the fireplace leaching the chill from her body. She turned her glass in her hand, watching as the gleam of firelight caught in the amber like some prehistoric insect.

The clock struck, giving her a start. Walter had said he would be home for dinner. She couldn't bear the thought of struggling through an evening with him. She dialed the restaurant, meaning to plead an excuse. She would say she was going to a movie with her mother, or perhaps that she had a headache and wanted to be alone.

None of which turned out to be necessary. A girlish young voice she didn't recognize informed her, 'Mr. Desmond isn't in today; it's his day off. Can I help you?'

She hung up without reply, relieved and puzzled at the same time. He had said he was going to the restaurant, hadn't he?

★   ★   ★

She was already in bed when she heard him come in. She listened, and concluded from his stumbling around and muttered remarks that he was drunk.

She got up to see if he needed help, but when she came near to the bedroom door, she heard him crying. She crept back to her own room, Becky's room, where she lay in the darkness and imagined, though it would have been impossible, that she could still hear his muted sobs.

★   ★   ★

At first, when she woke in the morning, she could not quite think what was different. She turned on her side and saw the glow of sunlight beaming into the bedroom. Going to the window, she pulled the curtains aside. The rain that had fallen for days had ended and the sky was blue and high above.

She was in the shower when she realized with a sense of discovery that something had happened to her. Something was different inside, in the very core of her being. She tried to analyze it, and came back to her meeting yesterday with Jack. It was as if that electrical shock of seeing him had jump-started her feelings, all the emotions she had so carefully locked away.

Out of nowhere, she began to cry — the first tears she had shed since that horrible moment in the parking lot, clinging to the door of a truck, fighting for her daughter.

She went to see her mother. She drove up Beverly Glen, seeing for the first time how green the hills were from all the rain, and took Mulholland Drive, following its twisted route across the ridge of hills that separate the valley from West L. A.

In the summer the valley would be thick with smog and visibility limited to no more than a few miles; but now, the air washed clean by rain, it spread out before her in all its immensity, seeming to go on and on forever before it collided with the purple-gray mountains in the distance.

Sandra, still in her bathrobe, was surprised to see her, and faintly alarmed, not sure what to expect. She had been worried since she had arrived at Dominique's yesterday and found Catherine gone. Several times she tried to phone, but there had been no answer. Now, suddenly, here Catherine was, stopped just inside the front door.

'It's funny,' Catherine said in the way of greeting, 'I was thinking that no matter where you have lived or for how long, coming to your mother's house is always 'coming home'.'

Sandra gave a timorous smile. 'Strange you should say that. I said almost the same words to your grandmother many years ago.'

'Oh, Mom,' Catherine said, and then they were in one another's arms, both of them crying and talking at the same time, and even laughing, and it was minutes before Sandra could steer them into the kitchen.

They sat at the little table there and had coffee and bagels and cried and laughed some more and after a while, to the great good pleasure of both, their chatter settled into the kind of frank, woman-to-woman conversation they had enjoyed so often together in the past.

'I've been so selfish,' Catherine said. 'I was so wrapped up in the pain of losing a daughter, I forgot that you had lost a granddaughter.'

'I felt as if I had lost a granddaughter and a daughter.' She made of it less a rebuke than a statement of fact.

'It's all right, really. I do understand,' Sandra said as she mopped up the coffee. 'When your father died — it's nearly ten years now — but I thought for a long time that my life was over. I simply couldn't imagine how I could go on without him.'

'It's so strange; you seemed at the time to be handling it so well.'

'I wasn't any better at sharing my pain than you have been. We're two of a kind, I suppose. The point is, time is the answer. It's such a cliché, but time is what does it.

It's early days yet. Wait, be patient, the wounds will heal. She'll never leave you, and that's all right too. It just won't hurt so much when you think of her. When I think of your father now, it's mostly with pleasure.'

'I think it's mostly the same for me.'

'You're thinking of Walter?'

Catherine looked directly at her mother. 'I was thinking of Jack McKenzie,' she said frankly.

'Oh.' Sandra sounded not particularly surprised.

'I seem to have loved him forever. And to have been unhappy about it nearly as long.'

'Oh, my dear, love has nothing to do with happiness. You can be quite happy with someone and not love him. And you can love him and despise him at the same time. I don't think once you love someone you can ever really stop loving, although you can certainly end the relationship.'

'I know I tried hard enough to get Jack out of my heart, but try though I will, he's still there.'

'I don't think I shall presume to advise

you on that score. You remember your Dante, don't you? When he first starts his journey it is Socrates, the intellect, who guides him; but when they reach a certain point, he turns the job over to Dante's beloved Beatrice. Which was Dante's way of saying, as I see it, there comes a time when reason be damned, you have to let your heart lead the way.'

★   ★   ★

She stopped at the mall again on her way home. At the entrance to Macy's Christmas department, she had to pause to steel herself. All the bustle, the noise, Christmas music piped over speakers, the babble of voices and the jangle of cash registers.

She made herself go in. She picked up two strings of lights, and got a third one for good measure. Four boxes of ornaments — that ought to be enough, wouldn't it? Tinsel, some garlands. She even got an angel for the treetop, and immediately named it Becky.

Those purchases made — and they

were the hardest — she went to men's and found a cashmere sweater for Walter; and to women's, where she picked out a Pashmina stole for her mother. She chose black first; and then, thinking that too funereal, traded it for a fire-engine red. But she could hear her mother saying, 'What on earth would I wear that with?' She settled finally for one in pale lilac.

She took her packages to gift-wrapping and had them wrapped. That, she decided, she still wasn't up to. Anyway, she had never been very good at it.

On her way home she stopped at her regular flower shop, Rose's Roses. They had ordered their Christmas trees from Rose Leiberman for years, always — Rose's little joke — calling it a Hanukkah bush.

The tinkle of the bell over the door and the familiar blend of flower-shop scents welcomed her. The pale blonde woman by the window was new to her, however. In the past Rose had always managed the shop alone. 'I was looking for Rose,' Catherine replied to her greeting.

'I'm here to help you,' the woman said.

A new employee, then. Catherine was

disappointed. She would have liked to see Rose herself, but Rose was getting on in years and the shop was probably too much for her to handle alone at this hectic time of year.

'I'd like to order a tree,' Catherine said.

'You must keep trying,' the woman said.

'Oh. You mean you don't have any trees this year?'

'Traveling is like a muscle: the more you use it, the stronger it gets,' was the puzzling response.

Catherine tried to digest that, but could make no sense of it. 'I'm sorry, I don't think I understand.' Did she know this woman? She looked vaguely familiar, but standing just in front of the window as she was, with the bright sunlight streaming in around her, it was difficult to make out her face. If one were fanciful one might almost imagine that the light made a halo about her head.

'I'm sorry about the pain, but it will get better too with practice. It does sort of go with the territory, unfortunately. You were shot in the head, after all.'

Catherine gasped. 'How could you possibly know . . . ?' she started to ask, taking a step towards this strange woman.

'Mrs. Desmond! Catherine!' Rose Leiberman came through the curtained doorway from the back room. 'What a wonderful surprise.'

Catherine turned to greet her and was swallowed up in a determined embrace, crushed against Rose's enormous bosom. 'I was so sorry, so very, very sorry,' Rose said. 'You poor darling.'

Catherine felt a cold draft across the back of her neck. It was a moment before she realized the shop door had opened and closed behind her. She jumped back and looked around. The woman had gone.

'Oh, wait,' she cried. She ran outside and looked up and down the street. The woman was nowhere to be seen.

Rose looked at her curiously when she came back in, the bell over the door jingling. 'Is something wrong?' she asked.

'That woman. She just disappeared. I wanted to talk to her. Did you know her?'

Rose looked around the shop, confused. 'Woman?'

'She was just there, by the window. She was talking to me when you came through the doorway.'

Rose looked in the direction of the window. 'Oh, I suppose she was just a looky-loo. We get them this time of year.' She dismissed the subject with a shrug and turned her friendly smile back to Catherine. 'Let me guess, you've come for a Hanukkah bush?'

4

At home, Catherine poured herself a glass of wine and, kicking off her shoes, curled up on the sofa in the den.

She could no longer ignore the fact that something downright weird was happening to her. But what, exactly? What had that woman at the flower shop meant, about traveling? Hadn't someone said the very same thing to her previously?

She tried to think back over all of it. The nightmare. On the face of it, there was nothing peculiar about that. Why wouldn't she have a nightmare about the men who had kidnapped her daughter?

What if it was *all* just a nightmare? What if she had in fact died when she was shot; and all the rest, everything that she had experienced since, was just some epic, drawn-out dream?

She tried to place things in some logical sequence. There had been that moment in the hospital when she had imagined herself in the hallway outside her room; and that must have seemed real to Millie, too, because remembering now that moment when the nurse burst into the room, recalling her expression, she realized that Millie had fully expected to see an empty bed. So Millie must have seen her in the corridor as well. Surely two people couldn't share the same delusion.

She thought about the woman doctor. Like the woman today at Rose's shop — they could have been the same person, she realized suddenly — the doctor, too, had mentioned travel. Had she been only a dream as well, or had she been real? Yes, of course she was real. She and Millie had exchanged words.

Or had they? The doctor had spoken, and Millie had spoken, but had they actually spoken to one another? She couldn't remember their exact words, but now she didn't think that they had.

Even that hadn't been the beginning, though. There was that eerie experience when she had been, if not dead, certainly dying. It had gotten blurry in her memory, like a faded photograph, and she had deliberately pushed that memory away. There had been light, she remembered that much — blinding light — and someone had spoken to her about a job to do. Something only she could do.

What had the woman in the shop said today — ? 'You must practice traveling.'

Okay, then, say that she had been 'traveling,' in some sense. Was she having what-did-they-call-them, out-of-body experiences?

Dean and Summers had published a book on paranormal experiences a few years back. She went to the bookshelves and found it, *An Almanac of the Paranormal*, and looked through the table of contents until she found a heading for 'astral projection.' Yes, that sounded like what had been happening to her.

She read for a moment and put the book down. It sounded like a lot of mumbo-jumbo, but she couldn't deny that something had happened to her; that she had traveled in some spirit fashion to other locations.

She had a chilling thought: if that

nightmare of her daughter's murderers was not a nightmare, then she had actually, spontaneously, traveled to where they were. Was that what she was meant to do — why she had been given this bizarre 'gift?' Because if so, God in heaven, she didn't want it.

Except, she hadn't been given any choice, had she? It *had* been spontaneous. But surely there must be some way to prevent that from happening again. She went back to the book. Yes, astral travelers generally learned with practice to control their projections; to choose where and when they would travel.

Well, then, there was the answer — practice, learn how to control it. Only, how was she supposed to practice something that occurred on its own? She didn't have any idea what she had done on any of those occasions; didn't in fact think that she had done anything to bring those weird experiences about.

'All right,' she said aloud, 'let's suppose I can travel, to borrow a word, and I just need to practice it. Let's pop in on Mom, why don't we?'

She made herself comfortable on the sofa, closed her eyes and concentrated hard, screwing up her face. Were there some magic words she was supposed to use? The book hadn't said. Abracadabra maybe?

After a while, feeling foolish, she opened her eyes. If she were supposed to practice this, they would have to give her some sort of hint as to how. Whoever, she amended, *they* were. And it would help if they explained why she was supposed to practice it. Much as she wanted to see them caught and put away, she did not want, ever, to pay any more visits to those two men.

The hall clock announced four. She remembered what Jack had said: channel three at four. Putting the book aside, she found the remote and flipped on the television to channel three, and there he was, talking about some problem with the Koreas. She watched him, paying no attention to his words, free now to study him without awkwardness.

He still had that odd mix of vulnerability and independence — the result, no doubt, of being orphaned young, of having to make his own way. Even as a young girl, she had wondered what lay within the still depths of those gray-blue eyes, keen eyes that seemed to look out from the screen straight into hers. She could almost feel herself falling into gray-blue pools. The light around him appeared golden, like a gilding fog . . .

Just like that, she was standing in an unfamiliar office, beside a desk.

★ ★ ★

'See if you can get me a ticket for the symphony for tonight,' Jack told his secretary as he passed her desk, barely slowing his brisk pace.

'The Chopin? 'Lang Lang'? I've heard it's sold out.'

'The peanut gallery will do. There's usually something up top.'

'One?' she asked after his rapidly vanishing back.

'One will be plenty.' He stepped into his office — and saw Catherine standing in front of his desk.

He blinked, and she was gone. Hadn't

really been there at all, of course; or if she had, it had only been a ghost, because he had seen the desk right through her.

★   ★   ★

Back in her den, Catherine looked for the daily newspaper. Yes, there it was, the Chopin First Piano Concerto, 'Lang Lang', with the Los Angeles Philharmonic Orchestra, tonight.

She smiled broadly. The Chopin First was the most romantic piece of music she knew. It was also, for her, intensely erotic. Jack had played it for her the night he first made love to her.

What did it say about him, that he was going tonight to listen to that very music? And what an uncanny coincidence it was that she had traveled to him at the very moment he told his secretary to find him a ticket.

Maybe there was an upside to this travel business. Smiling, she dialed her mother's telephone number. 'Mom,' she said, 'do you still have your symphony subscription?'

'Yes, although I hardly ever go. As a matter of fact, now that you mention it, I have tickets for tonight and I can't make it. It's bridge night. Did you want them?'

★ ★ ★

She promised herself that she wouldn't actually speak to him, wouldn't even meet up with him. She only wanted to see him, to know that she was under the same roof with him, sharing the same musical experience.

Nonetheless, here she was, standing in the lobby near the main entrance, waiting to see him arrive. As usual, he was late. The lobby began to empty as people ascended the stairs on their way to the auditorium. She shifted her weight from one foot to another and gingerly sipped a glass of wine.

What if he didn't come? He might have changed his mind. Or his secretary might have been unable to find a ticket.

She set her wine aside on the bar and started toward the escalator — and stopped dead as Jack dashed in, at the last minute, just as always in the past; she ought to have remembered that. Wind-blown and coatless, a man who couldn't deign to notice the weather, he hurried into the lobby.

Her promises to herself went out the door as he came in. She took a deep breath, put her head down, and moved in a path that would intercept his, walking quickly. Already the smartly uniformed usher was holding out her hand to scan his ticket.

'Jack.' She looked directly at him at the last minute. 'This is a surprise.'

'Catherine.' He gave her a measuring look, as if he were not altogether as surprised as she professed to be.

She managed a warm smile. 'The Chopin,' was all she could say.

'Yes. It's one of my favorites.' He looked down at his watch. 'We'd better get inside.'

The usher scanned their tickets, and realized belatedly that there were three tickets and only two people, but Catherine was past her and already moving up the escalator before she could say anything. She shrugged, and turned instead to another late arrival.

Catherine waited until they had almost reached the next level before she asked, 'Where are you sitting?' She tried to make the question innocent.

He grimaced and nodded his head upward. 'The top. Nose-bleed country.'

'But, no, I have an extra seat right beside me. Mother was supposed to come and changed her mind at the last minute. Orchestra. Why don't you join me?'

They had reached the orchestra level. 'That's very kind of you, but . . . '

'Please,' she interrupted him. 'You did say we were going to be friends, didn't you? And I really hate going in by myself.'

He looked at his watch again. By now they were very nearly alone.

'I insist.' She put a hand on his arm and steered them toward the door to the auditorium.

★   ★   ★

He could barely concentrate on the music, so aware was he of Catherine next to him. Their arms brushed and he jerked his away as if it had been burned.

Probably she had forgotten the last time they heard this together, but that evening was branded on his soul.

It was over at last. They drifted out of the auditorium with the crowd. There was another selection, Liszt, to follow the intermission; but as if it had already been discussed, they took the escalator down to the lobby, went past the little gift shop and out the exit. Neither had any interest in staying now that what they had come to hear was over.

They stopped on the veranda. The night was balmy, a gentle breeze chasing the clouds. She looked up at a starlit sky, at the swooping stainless-steel wings of the concert hall that seemed to embrace them.

'Where are you parked?' Jack asked.

'Downstairs. You parked at the Chandler?'

'Yes. I'll see you to your car.'

Neither of them made a move to go, however. After another long silence, she asked, 'Where are you living now?'

'I found a little place in Santa Monica. Tiny, but if you lean far enough out the bathroom window you can get a glimpse of the ocean before you fall.'

She smiled, and then surprised even herself by saying, 'Can we go there?'

He sighed and she knew before he said it what the answer would be. 'I don't think that would be a good idea.' Did she really think that, in the privacy of his own apartment, alone with her, he would be able to keep his hands off her? Or was she just mocking him?

Her heart sank. 'No, you're probably right.' She managed to shape her lips into a semblance of a smile at the same time she was mentally kicking herself. Why did she insist on making this fool of herself over him? Hadn't he already made it clear that the past was over and buried? 'Well, goodnight, then.'

She started to leave and, pausing, turned back to where he stood. 'Would it be all right if I called you sometime? It really would be nice to think we could still be friends. I think I need friends just now.'

'Absolutely. I'd like that.' He found a business card in his wallet and scribbled hastily on the back of it, and handed it to her.

She tucked it into her pocket without

looking at it and with a final quick nod, left him.

★ ★ ★

Driving home amidst the river of cars on the freeway, the lighted towers of the city gliding past, her thoughts turned inevitably, despairingly, to her latest meeting with Jack. What if he were involved with someone else? He had been alone tonight, but that didn't necessarily negate the possibility. Part of her knew that, sensibly, it might well be best for him, for both of them, if he were involved with someone.

At home she left the Jaguar in the driveway and, before she got out, took his card from her pocket and glanced at it. He had written not only his phone number, but his address as well.

A Freudian slip? Or a deliberate invitation? Her spirits, sunk in a pit a moment before, soared toward the heavens. She put the card carefully into her purse and slid smiling out of the car and turned a little pirouette on the flagstone walk. She felt drunk, and not on the glass of wine she'd had earlier, but on something far headier.

For better or for worse, she was — still — head over heels in love with Jack McKenzie. And just at the moment, she couldn't begin to imagine how she was going to deal with that truth. It was enough for now to have faced it without any pretense.

She started up the walk, but halfway to the front door she stopped abruptly, the hair on the nape of her neck rising. She had a sense of someone near, someone or something evil.

She turned around in a circle, looking. The halogen lights made the front lawn as bright as day. There was no one to be seen, and yet the sense of a threatening presence remained.

A stonewall and a row of citrus trees — a lemon, an orange, a grapefruit, neatly spaced — shielded the lawn from the street. There were shadows there among the trees, but no sign of any prowler lurking in them.

Frightened, not knowing quite why, she hurried to the front door.

* * *

In a seedy cottage a few miles away, Lester Paterson — Trash Can to those who knew him — woke abruptly, his eyes flying open.

It was her, that woman again. He stared upward into the darkness. On the nearby sofa, J. D. Colley snored loudly.

Who was she, and why was she popping into his mind this way, like a ghost? Not even into his mind, exactly; more like she was actually here, close by. He had a feeling that if he sat up and looked, he would see her across the room, the way he had that other time.

Of one thing he was certain: whoever she was, she was a threat to him. One that he had to eliminate. Fast.

5

Sunday morning dawned warm and sunny. Catherine woke with a feeling of resolve. She had decided before she fell asleep last night that there were things that she must do, and first among those was one she would do right away — before she got cold feet.

She had determined to shed that wearisome past that had weighted her down for far too long now. Like the spoiled child who will eat nothing because he cannot have the apple pie he demands, she had cursed life because it was not what it had been before.

Well, it wasn't ever going to be. She had no idea what future lay hidden in the golden light from the window, but of one thing she was sure: she must make it for herself.

Walter was in the kitchen, sipping coffee and reading the morning paper. She waited until she had poured herself a cup of coffee before she interrupted him.

'I'm going to leave,' she said without preamble. 'Today.'

His hand paused with the cup halfway to his mouth, sniffed and looked up at her for a long measuring moment. 'You mean permanently?'

'Yes. I mean a divorce. I'm sorry. I don't blame you any longer for what happened, and I know you have your own pain to bear. But it's never going to be right again between us, Walter. Maybe it never was.'

He sighed. 'I won't make any problems. However you want to arrange it. I'll divorce you if you prefer. But you don't have to leave, you know. I can move out and you can keep the house. Without you, without . . . it's nothing to me.'

She shook her head and made an expansive gesture that took in the kitchen and beyond, the entire house. 'No, I want to go. I don't want to remain here. This place is too loaded with baggage. If I had been wise, I wouldn't have come back here at all.'

He looked around as if seeing for the

first time the house they had lived in nearly all the years of their marriage. 'Then we'll sell it and split whatever we get. When . . . Today, did you say?'

'I don't see any point in putting it off. I'll get a hotel room for now, just take a few personal items with me. The rest can go into storage till I have an apartment.'

'Leave it here. I'll stay till we get it sold; and when you're ready, I'll get your things moved. Like I said, I won't make any trouble. You don't have to worry about that.'

To her surprise, he returned his attention to his newspaper. She felt an odd sense of disappointment. Of course, she had hoped that he would take her announcement well. It was only that she hadn't expected such total disinterest.

She managed a grateful smile. 'I appreciate your being so reasonable, Walter, really I do. You've been kind. You've been a good husband in so many ways. I just . . . ' She shrugged. 'I just want to free myself of the past.'

He looked up at her briefly, seemed on the verge of saying something and then, changing his mind, smiled wanly. It occurred to her that perhaps he knew of her love for Jack McKenzie; knew that Jack was a part of why she wanted a divorce.

She could do nothing to ease that pain for him, however. She had no idea if Jack still wanted her; would ever want her again the way he had before. But of one thing she was certain: he would never have her so long as she remained attached to someone else. Quite possibly not even then, but she had to try. She had thought that through clearly last night, lying in bed.

Walter nodded again. 'I understand,' he said.

★   ★   ★

She went that same morning to the Sportsman's Lodge on Ventura Boulevard and got a room overlooking the swans in the pond outside. By early afternoon she had unpacked her single bag, had arranged a small pile of books by the nightstand and her laptop on the little table, and placed the single framed picture of Becky atop the dresser. She looked around at the cookie-cutter room and thought wryly, 'Home sweet home.'

Only until she found an apartment. She had taken the room for a week, sure that in that time span she could find something that suited her. She wasn't too particular; she needed nothing more than the basics: a reasonably functional kitchen — she wasn't much of a cook — a bath, a bedroom, and someplace to sit down and prop up her feet.

She had a late lunch in the lodge's dining room, glanced through rental listings in the *Sunday Times*, highlighting one or two, and went back to her room. She had brought *An Almanac of the Paranormal* with her and, kicking off her shoes, she turned again to the section on astral projection.

That was another of last night's resolutions: since it seemed she had somehow acquired this dubious gift, and since she was being prodded to use it, it behooved her to learn a little more about it and see if she could get any clearer on what it was she was supposed to do.

The book, unfortunately, was big on generalities and short on specifics. Most of those who 'projected' themselves did so in visible form, though others learned to do so invisibly. Few of them had any corporeal presence. Not physical themselves, they could not move objects; nor did the people they visited feel their physical touch. Some, though, did find a way to 'touch' people mentally, to make their presence felt.

All very interesting, and clearly those were aspects of her 'gift' she would need to work on. Unfortunately, the writer offered no instructions on how to do any of these things. She sighed and closed the book, putting it aside on the nightstand. She would have to find her own way, it seemed.

She thought back over her previous experiences; simply willing herself to go somewhere hadn't worked. What had she done when she popped into Jack's office? She had been just thinking about him, hadn't she? Had seen him on the television screen, looked into his eyes, *gone* into his eyes in some sense. Visiting

Jack was all well and good, of course, but that was too easy. There had always been a bond between them, a spiritual connection if you wanted to put it that way, but she had a notion that wasn't why this ability had been presented to her.

On the other hand, she didn't exactly relish a visit to her two nemeses, though a part of her had begun to understand that this might well be the point of it all — but not, please, until she had gotten a better idea how to handle these 'trips.' No more horrible scenes to witness unprepared. Especially, she did not want them to see her. She did not want, really, *ever* want to see that man's eyes on her again.

She thought of Walter. Yes, that would be harmless. She could try making herself invisible and if he should see her, he would almost certainly think it a product of his imagination. She closed her eyes, relaxing, and conjured up an image of their house; saw Walter's face, familiar and yet in some ways utterly a stranger's face —   and as easily as that, found herself standing just inside the door of his home office.

For a moment, she thought that he wasn't there, that she had somehow alighted in the wrong spot. Then she saw him, kneeling on the floor beyond his desk. She looked past him and saw to her surprise an opening in the floor of the closet that she had not known was there, a cubbyhole. He was just putting something into it and, as she watched, he replaced the flooring and pulled the turned-back carpet into place over that.

She remembered what she had just read: there, but not seen. All right, then, that was certainly what was needed for this situation. Only how did you . . . and discovered that it was far easier than she would have imagined. It was like dialing down the volume on the radio. She could feel herself fade, even as the room before her seemed to mist over. She still saw everything, but it was like seeing it through a veil of gauze.

Make yourself felt? She had no clue how one did that either. She stared hard at the back of Walter's head and mentally called his name.

Suddenly he froze, cocking his head as

if he had heard something. Or felt her standing behind him.

'Catherine?' he called aloud and turned in her direction — and looked right through her. There was no indication in his expression that he had seen her at all. His puzzled gaze swept the room, came back to where she was standing, and went about the room once again.

Jackpot, she thought triumphantly, and the next instant was back in her room at The Sportsman's Lodge, her head throbbing. He hadn't seen her, and of that she was glad. She hadn't intended to spy on him. He had a right to his privacy, after all.

She couldn't help wondering about that cubbyhole though, and what he had been hiding in it. Again she realized how little she knew the man with whom she had lived until today. Pornography? Drugs? Perhaps a cache of money and the makings of another identity? She had read of men who maintained marriages to two or sometimes more different women, different families and careers.

No, she couldn't imagine Walter with

another wife. He had barely had the energy or the interest for one.

Or, she thought, perhaps she simply hadn't been the right one. A blow to the ego, that idea; but her disinterest in him, in much of their relationship, might have been the very mirror of his feelings. People married what they needed. She had married Walter out of spite, and out of a now outdated convention that said women were supposed to marry. Mistakes, both.

But why had he married her? She had always supposed that it was because of his ardent love for her, and wasn't that flattering to her? It hadn't been ardent, however, not for a very long time. Not even, if she were to be completely honest, at the beginning. There had always been something perfunctory about their physical relations.

Why on earth had he married her, then? Or, more accurately, what was it that he had needed of her? Because, surely, she hadn't provided it all these years. She couldn't pretend that to herself.

She thought again of that hidey-hole in his office that he had kept secret from her for heaven knew how long. She could poke into it, of course. Not in her astral form: as a spirit she couldn't move the box or lift the floorboards. She would have to visit the house at some time, though, to pack up her things. It was tempting to imagine taking a peek into this obviously most private part of his life, to learn what secret he thought it necessary to conceal from her.

No, the bottom line was, it was none of her business. Even though they were not yet divorced, had not even begun proceedings, she had settled in her mind as of the night before that they were no longer man and wife.

Leave it, she told herself. She changed into her sweats. Another of her resolutions had been to get herself back into shape, starting with a daily run. After that, she would check out a few apartments.

★　★　★

By Tuesday she had found an apartment, in what she would have regarded as the least likely of all places.

It started when Bill, her young assistant, paused in her doorway to say, 'I understand you're looking for a place to live?'

'Word gets around quickly, doesn't it?' She looked up from the mountain of work covering her desk.

'Oh — I wasn't gossiping, if that's what you mean. I just . . . ' He fumbled for words. 'Well, what I stopped to tell you is, there's this apartment in my building. I took the liberty of checking it out. I wouldn't have wanted to recommend some dump to you.'

'And?'

He grinned. 'It's really cute, actually. I'd snatch it up myself, except it's out of my range.' His grin faded a little. 'Of course, you can't always tell what someone else will like. It may not suit you at all. But if you want, I'll call Jan — that's my landlord. He's pretty particular about who he takes in, so he hasn't actually advertised the place yet.

He prefers word of mouth.'

Catherine cast a dubious eye at the pile of galleys scattered across her desk. On the other hand, she did need to find an apartment, and the sooner the better. And Bill's remark had been rather in the nature of a compliment, hadn't it?

'Do, please,' she said. 'This afternoon, if it's convenient.'

When she discovered that the apartment was smack-dab in the middle of West Hollywood — L.A.'s gay neighborhood — she almost got back into the car without even looking at the apartment; but she reminded herself that Bill had taken the trouble to make an appointment with his apparently quite particular landlord.

Who turned out to be a tall, spare man of fifty-something, wearing a billowing silver caftan and one dangly brass earring. He was olive-skinned and had a large nose — Arabic, she thought, or perhaps Greek. Jan. Janos?

'It's the top floor, and no elevator,' Jan said in a whisky baritone, leading the way up steep, narrow stairs that creaked in faint concert with the swish of his caftan. 'My legs resent it, but my butt is grateful.'

He opened the door for her and stepped aside to let her enter first. She came directly into a small living room whose high, beamed ceiling made it seem larger than it was. Huge windows welcomed in every ray of the pale winter sunlight. There was a well-used fireplace in the wall facing her, and a one-person balcony in front, overlooking Santa Monica Boulevard.

It was love at first sight. She strolled into the smallish bedroom, the even smaller but efficient-looking kitchen, and the surprisingly enormous bathroom. It was not a lot of space overall, but that just meant she would have less furniture to buy. Back in the living room, she indicated an expensive-looking leather sofa that sat alone against one wall. 'Bill didn't mention furnishings.'

'The previous tenant's. She needed money for airfare, so I gave her cash for it, in the hopes that the next person might want it. If not, I'll have it hauled away. Or it's yours for two hundred.'

'Sold.' She wrote a check, he gave her a set of keys, and they shook hands.

'I hope you'll be happy here,' he said with a grin that flashed a sea of white teeth, and left her standing in the middle of her new home. She turned around slowly, wondering for a second or two if she had been too quick, and deciding that she was entirely happy with her decision.

The little balcony overlooked Santa Monica Boulevard itself, but on the top of three floors it was high enough to escape much of the noise and the smell of auto fumes. And the bedroom was to the back, which meant it should be quiet enough for sleeping.

She checked out of the lodge and went shopping. She bought a lamp and a mini-stereo for the living room, and ordered a bed and dresser delivered, and a small television for the bedroom. She imagined herself lying in bed watching Jack on the TV, though why she should be lying in bed at four in the afternoon she hadn't yet worked out.

She called Rose to have the Hanukkah bush delivered to her new address instead of the house, and thought about ordering a second one for Walter, but decided he probably wouldn't care. Probably wouldn't even notice, truth to tell.

Some linen, a coffee-maker and some freshly ground coffee — her idea of roughing it was a morning without coffee. Some juice and some cereal and some milk.

Wheeling her cart through Gelson's, she had a last-minute inspiration and added some Beefeaters, a bottle of Noilly Prat and some olives to her cart. By five o'clock that evening she was standing on her little balcony sipping a martini and watching a drooping sun trying to cast its evening colors on an uncooperatively gray sky and managing only a pallid mauve for its efforts.

She finished the martini and, deciding to skip dinner, kicked off her shoes and made a bed of sorts on the leather sofa. She toyed with Jack's business card for a moment before putting it back in her purse. The light off, she took a final breath of air on her balcony, and thought of his description of his apartment: if you leaned out far enough, you had a glimpse of the ocean before you fell.

Santa Monica was to the west. She looked in that direction as though, if she leaned out far enough and looked hard enough, she might get a glimpse of him. There was nothing more pathetic than those foolish souls who lived altogether in the past, wasting their todays in pursuit of their yesterdays. It was a very human folly to wish something to be that was not, and sadly there were those who lived their entire lives in pursuit of what would never be.

Yet she truly felt as if fortune had handed her a second go-round with Jack. He had walked mysteriously, miraculously back into her life at the very time when she was most prepared to realize the emptiness of her marriage to Walter.

She went in, carefully locking the balcony door, and settled herself on the sofa for her first night in her new home.

6

'You've rented an apartment in boy's town?' Sandra sounded genuinely surprised.

'It's a very diverse community, mother.' Catherine switched the phone to her other hand as she inked a contract.

'Oh I know — I love it. I just somehow never imagined you there. You've always been a bit . . . ' She hesitated.

'Prissy?' Catherine suggested. Fermin had once, over a lunch with one too many cocktails, described her that way and it was a word she had sometimes since applied to herself in more critical moments.

'Sheltered, I think, is the word I would use. Self-possessed. You've always stood at the castle window looking down at life, dear. I should think that would be a bit more difficult in such a vibrant neighborhood.'

'What an extraordinary thing to say.'

Catherine stared at the phone in annoyance.

'But true. Things have happened in your life, some good, some terrible, but they have always happened *to* you, never *by* you, darling. When it comes to the business of living, you've just never gotten down and dirty. Yes, now that I think of it, West Hollywood might be just the place for you.'

'I'm glad you approve.' If her mother noticed her sarcasm, she gave no sign of it.

'And there is one upside to consider, as a woman now living alone: if a strange man bursts into your apartment, he's more likely to be interested in your dresses than your body.'

'Not funny, mother.'

Her mother was unrepentant.

★   ★   ★

She bought Bill a bottle of Dom Perignon as a thank-you. Even if he wasn't into wine, that was a safe bet.

Maybe her mother was right. She

88

pondered that in the ladies' room. The last really decisive action she had taken in her life had been marrying Walter. From the day she had taken that plunge, she had been treading water.

No, she corrected herself. That was no longer true. The *last* decisive action had been leaving Walter — and maybe that meant she was truly on the mend.

She turned to look at herself in the mirror and as she did, the lights brightened, as if someone had turned a rheostat up. For a startled moment she thought she saw someone in the glass behind her, but when she looked over her shoulder there was no one there.

You must go to them. The voice seemed to be inside her head.

'Them?' Catherine said aloud. It took her a moment to understand. 'Those men? No, no, I can't, I won't.'

There's another little girl. Debbie will suffer a living hell. You must stop them.

'But how can I? I can't. There's nothing I can do,' Catherine cried, but it was too late. Her image in the glass faded into the golden glow, the light seemed to explode, blinding, scorching . . .

'Excuse me, ma'am.'

She was in a department store — Nieman's, she thought. The man in front of her said, 'I wonder if you could help me with something?'

She started to reply, and realized he was not looking at her at all. He was looking through her. Literally. She suddenly realized who he was. She'd had only glimpses of him before, and then he was always unkempt. Now his hair was neatly trimmed and he was clean-shaven. He wore chinos and an expensive-looking leather jacket over a burgundy turtleneck. He might have been any one of the hundreds of unaccompanied males in the store for Christmas shopping.

For all the pains he had taken to clean himself up, however, he was unquestionably Yellow Beard's companion, the one she thought of as the Bear. And he was speaking to someone behind her.

Heart racing, she looked over her shoulder at a matron dressed all in blue: a navy coat, a sky-blue dress, turquoise shoes and purse. Even her pewter hair had highlights of blue in it. She pawed through a rack of blouses while at her side a young girl of maybe ten or eleven fidgeted impatiently.

'Mommy, can't we go?' the girl asked.

'In a moment, Debbie.' The mother looked in the Bear's direction. 'Yes?' she answered him a bit coolly.

Catherine stepped back to watch. The Bear held up a sweater in one hand and a scarf in the other and gave Lady Blue a sheepish grin. 'I'm no good at this kind of thing,' he said, his expression oozing an oafish sincerity. 'I'm looking for presents for my wife, but I don't know, do these colors look right together?'

'Oh.' Lady Blue's smile was warmer now. She looked doubtfully at the avocado-green sweater and the nearly chartreuse scarf. 'Is she fond of green?' she asked.

'Well, now you mention it . . . ' He screwed up his face for a moment, seemed to notice her costume for the first time, and grinned, a warm and thoroughly convincing grin. 'I think she wears blue a lot more than green.'

She nodded. 'Ah. Let's look at what

they have in blue, why don't we?' She turned toward the display of sweaters and he turned with her — and managed, Catherine saw, to place himself between her and her daughter.

Mother and stranger began to discuss sweaters, holding them up for one another's inspection. This one she liked, but got a shake of his head. 'Don't look like her.' He offered an alternative and she pursed her lips before deciding against it and offering another.

Debbie began to drift away. She paused to look at a mannequin in a pink taffeta gown and looked back at where her mother was still earnestly engaged in conversation with the stranger. She wandered a few feet further.

Debbie will suffer a living hell . . .

No, Catherine thought with sudden determination. She hadn't wanted this, did not want to be here; but here she was, and clearly she was meant to stop what was obviously a kidnapping in progress.

But how? she wondered. And where was Yellow Beard? Surely he could not be far away. Her eyes scanned the crowds.

A man stepped from behind a column. At first, her anxious gaze went right on past him, but something clicked, and she looked again. It was him, Yellow Beard — only the beard had been shaved off, just as in her dream. His hair, long and yellow and straggly before, was a medium brown now, short and as nicely cut as his partner's.

It was his face that had changed the most, however. The mole was definitely gone. In its place she could see only a faint mark where it had been. What she hadn't fully noticed in that previous brief vision of him, however, was his nose. That, too, was different, straight where before it had been decidedly bent. It was a face etched permanently in her mind, but if she had only that police picture to go by, she might have walked right by him in a busy department store and never have noticed him.

Any doubts she might have had faded entirely when she looked into his eyes. Even knowing he could not see her, she felt a chill of fear. The evil in those eyes was unchanged. Eyes trained on little

Debbie like a hawk's, watching her edge ever closer to him. And closer to the door that led into the mall, where a man and a small girl could be lost in minutes in the teeming crowd of shoppers.

Catherine looked back at the child's mother, still oblivious to her daughter's straying. She stared hard at the back of the mother's head, willing the woman to feel her presence, her energy. It had worked with Walter, once, in the quiet of his office — but would it work in a crowded department store, with a stranger who was engaged in earnest conversation?

For long, agonizing seconds, it seemed as if nothing were happening. Catherine worried over the child, wondering if she had drifted any closer to Yellow Beard; but she dare not look, dare not risk a break in her concentration. In frustration, she decided that she must, after all, let herself be seen. She moved into the woman's line of sight.

Suddenly, the mother frowned and glanced around. 'Debbie?' she called, and then more loudly, 'Debbie, where are you?'

'I'm right here, mother,' Debbie called back.

'Don't you be wandering off. You get right back here. Haven't I told you never to go off like that? You gave me a fright.'

'I was just looking around.' Debbie returned obediently to her mother, who stooped down to tug an errant scarf into place around her daughter's neck and brush a sandy curl back from her forehead.

'You just stay right here beside mommy, that's a good girl. We'll go in a minute. Now, as I was saying . . . ' But when she straightened and turned back toward her shopping student, he was gone. She looked around, puzzled, but he had vanished.

★   ★   ★

Trash Can Paterson moved quickly, carefully, through the holiday crowds, showing no outward sign of the anger that raged within him. Ahead of him Cooley walked hurriedly toward the exit and the van waiting in the parking lot. Neither of

95

them took any notice of the other.

Paterson swore over and over to himself. A woman, arms filled with packages, stopped just in front of him. He resisted the urge to shove her aside and stepped around her instead. *Don't call attention.* It was his mantra on these shopping expeditions. Attention could be fatal.

She had been there, he was certain of it, even though he hadn't actually seen her. He had felt her as sure as if she had been standing alongside him. It was she who had interfered in some way that he couldn't quite figure out.

Who was she? He had to find her.

★　★　★

'Hey.'

Catherine jumped and looked up to see Fermin Dean in her doorway. 'Sorry, didn't mean to scare you,' he said. 'Are you all right? You look like you've seen a ghost.'

She wondered briefly what he would think if she said she had. Probably he would think she was losing her marbles. He might be right.

'Just a little on edge,' she said.

'I'm buying some of the boys a Christmas drink at the Polo Lounge. Care to join us?'

She was on the verge of declining, but she wasn't sure that she wanted to be alone just now. Maybe a room full of convivial people was what she needed.

'I would love to,' she said instead. 'If I really can be just one of the boys.'

Fermin laughed. 'Well, yes, but let it be said, you look lots better in a dress than the others.'

★   ★   ★

Jack, who didn't much like parties to begin with, glanced for the umpteenth time at his watch and wondered yet again if it was still too early to leave. He would rather have not come at all; but when the station's owner rents a suite at the Beverly Hills Hotel for a Christmas party, one did have a degree of obligation. Particularly when Peter Weitman had specifically asked him to attend.

'The boss asked for you in particular,' was how he had put it, which did make the obligation a bit weightier. Peter had given him his job, after all, and if he could repay the favor in some measure by sipping a weak Chivas-and-water and listening to some not-very-amusing banter, it seemed the least he could do.

'You wouldn't be thinking of slipping away, would you?' someone said beside him.

He turned toward the voice. Kitty Fane, the station's new weatherperson, regarded him with eyes both amused and speculative. They had been introduced briefly before and he had watched her initial performance on the monitor in his office. She was pretty in a reedy way, though personally he liked his women with a little more substance than she carried on her slight frame. Her hair was auburn and the eyes gazing into his were green and large, made larger still by generous shading of brown and green. The hand she laid on his arm sported black fingernails.

'Because if you are,' she said with a smile, 'I do wish you would take me with you. This is a bit of a bore, isn't it?'

'You wouldn't want the old man to hear you say that,' he cautioned.

She threw a quick look over her shoulder, but the nearest party guests were several feet away and engrossed in their own conversations.

She smiled back at Jack. 'Well, were you?' she asked.

'Leaving?' He glanced again at his watch. 'I think it's a bit early yet for that. And here he comes, by the way.' Peter Weitman and Thaddeus Tremayne — the old man — were making their way through the cocktail party crowd that, like the Red Sea, parted before them.

Kitty drew her shoulders back like a boxer entering the ring, making her small breasts more prominent in the shimmering emerald-green dress she wore, and turned to greet the newcomers, her smile wide.

Weitman did the introductions. Kitty laid it on a bit thick, Jack thought. 'I can't tell you what a thrill this is,' she said, holding Tremayne's hand a trifle longer than was necessary.

Jack saw that Thaddeus Tremayne was no more immune to flattery from an attractive woman than any other man, but he had a solid reputation too as a hard-headed businessman. After a few chatty remarks, he said, 'I wanted to have a few words with this young man, if you'll excuse us.'

Kitty made a moue of disappointment. 'Of course, but I insist on equal time.' She flashed a coy smile and moved in the direction of the bar.

'Pretty.' Tremayne watched her walk away from them, emerald-clad hips swaying provocatively.

When he turned his gaze to Jack, it was all business, however. 'I told Peter I particularly wanted a chance to meet you. I wanted to tell you that we've been getting lots of really good feedback on the pieces you've done.'

Behind him, Weitman wore a pleased-as-punch grin. Jack, after all, had been his find. He gave Jack a quick wink.

'I'm glad to hear it,' Jack said, 'but I

hope you'll understand if I say I'd like to think some of it was negative. My goal is to get people thinking for themselves, and if they're all parroting my opinions I'm not doing my job.'

'Then I can tell you that there is enough disagreement to assure that your job is being done nicely, and no more than just enough. I especially liked that piece last week on the Middle East.'

'That's one area, at least, where we don't have to worry about everyone agreeing.'

'Just so.' Tremayne smiled benevolently and looked at someone over Jack's head, a signal that Jack took to mean their conversation was finished. 'Keep up the good work. And I think you'll find a pleasant surprise in your next pay check.'

Jack could only mutter a quick thanks, but Tremayne was already on his way with a brief dismissive nod.

His reason for coming having been accomplished, Jack thought it was probably safe to start planning his exit. He did a brief tour of the room, stopping here and there to chat with a colleague, and declining the offer of a fresh drink from a black-jacketed waiter with a tray. Within the half-hour he was slipping into his well-traveled trenchcoat, but before he made it out the door a hand grabbed his arm and he looked down at black fingernails.

'Do take me with you, please.' Kitty glanced up at him with one of her most alluring smiles. 'I so hate to be seen leaving a party alone.'

'I'm sure there is not a man here who wouldn't happily solve that problem for you,' he said gallantly, but he fetched her coat for her and helped her into it. 'I thought you were going to have a conversation with the old man.'

Her smile this time was conspiratorial and just a trifle smug, which told more clearly than words that it had been, in her terms, a successful conversation. 'Mission accomplished,' she said.

They exchanged nothing more than some desultory remarks as they rode the elevator down, but when they exited through the lobby doors to the wide front steps, where he had supposed they would part, she held on to his arm. 'I have a bottle of Moet Chandon in the fridge, if you'd like to stop by,' she said. 'And I'm practically just around the corner.'

'I'll have to skip that corner this evening.' As gently as he could, he freed his arm. 'Previous engagement.' She needn't know that it was with a Graham Green novel.

'One that can't be broken?' She arched an eyebrow but he gave her an apologetic grimace. 'Then you'll have to take a rain check,' she said with a weatherperson's undiminished cheeriness.

She handed him a scrap of paper from the pocket of her sable. He glanced and saw that she had already written her number on it. Miss Fane liked to be prepared, apparently, for any eventuality.

'Call me.' The invitation in her eyes hinted at more than a glass of wine.

★ ★ ★

Pulling into the long, sweeping driveway of the Beverly Hills Hotel, Catherine wondered, not for the first time, how it was possible that all of the young valet parkers could be so movie-star gorgeous. The one dashing toward her Jaguar could have stepped right off the big screen.

She was half in, half out of the car when she glanced toward the lobby doors, where the wide steps swept down to the driveway, and saw Jack McKenzie coming out of the hotel with a stunning redhead on his arm. He turned so that his back was toward Catherine, but there was no mistaking the look the redhead slanted up at him.

Disappointment — and jealousy, no point pretending to oneself — stabbed at her. *Well, what did you expect?* she demanded angrily of herself. *It's not as if he's taken the vows or anything. He's a man, dammit. And trust him to pick a beautiful companion. Beautiful, if a trifle obvious.*

The tow-headed valet held the door wide for her and gave her a smile that would have done a toothpaste commercial proud. She shook her head, biting her lip to avert the tears that threatened, fumbled in her purse for a twenty-dollar bill, and thrust it into the waiting hand.

'Sorry, I've changed my mind.' She gave her head a shake.

She was already driving forward by the time he swung the door closed for her. She kept her head turned, hoping that Jack wouldn't see her, until she was going down the other end of the curved driveway, and in a minute more she was merging into the traffic on Sunset Boulevard, where she could safely brush a tear away from her cheek.

★　★　★

Watching her tail-lights disappear, Jack cursed Kitty Fane, still smiling up at him, for her would-be seduction.

'Is something wrong? You looked so funny for a minute,' she said.

No, that wasn't fair. It wasn't Kitty's fault — wasn't anyone fault, as far as that went. It was just damned bad luck was all.

'Sorry,' he said apologetically. 'I was just thinking of something.'

'I hope you were reconsidering that champagne.'

He flirted with that temptation only briefly, however. He had a notion that Kitty's charm, thin as it was already, would grow a lot thinner in the course of an evening. He wanted more from a woman than what she was so obviously offering, and he doubted very much that she had it to give.

'Sorry. Afraid it's not in the cards. Well, good night now,' he said and was off down the steps, signaling for one of the valets, before she could offer any further enticements.

7

Back in her apartment, Catherine changed into jeans and an oversized cashmere pullover, poured a glass of wine, and settled into a serious bout of floor pacing. She berated herself for a fool for not having called Jack before this; raged at him for his infidelity — never mind that he had no reason to practice fidelity; and found the world in general and all things upon it to be wanting. She had, in short, a wonderful session of feeling sorry for herself.

Having drained the wine glass and much of her emotion, she picked up the phone, found Jack's card and violently punched in his number.

He was surprised, certainly, to hear her voice. 'Am I interrupting?' she asked a shade too sweetly. 'You do have company, I take it?'

'In a manner of speaking.' Was that amusement in his voice?

'Then she will just have to listen. There

107

are some things I want to say.'

'That's not a problem,' Jack said. 'And it's a he, by the way. Graham Greene.'

'Oh. But I thought . . . I saw . . . ' Some of the wind went out of her sails.

'She was just a colleague,' he said patiently. 'We left the station bash — attendance obligatory, or I wouldn't have been there at all — walked out together, and we parted company just about the time you escaped down the drive.'

Feeling like an utter fool, she blurted out the first thing that came into her mind. 'Have you had dinner?'

'I was just eyeing a can of tuna. Without much enthusiasm, I might add. Why don't I pick you up? I know a place I think you'll love.'

'I'm in jeans.'

'Perfect. So am I. And you can say all those things you wanted to say over dinner,' he added.

* * *

She saved him the difficult chore of finding a parking place by saying she would wait for him at the curb. If he was surprised to hear that she was living at a new address, he saved his questions for later as well.

He was there in less than half an hour, a honk of his horn alerting her as the silver-gray Porsche glided to a stop. She jumped in with a quick nervous grin and fidgeted with her seat belt to give herself a moment's grace.

'I should explain,' she began, but he interrupted her.

'Dinner first. Explanations after. It makes for a much nicer evening. And I think we can treat ourselves to one of those, can't we?'

Why had she thought this would be so difficult? Nothing in the intervening years had felt more natural than that she should be sitting beside him in his car as they wound their way up Laurel Canyon into the Valley, engine purring, Maxine Sullivan's honeyed voice insinuating itself into the comfortable silence. It had rained earlier, briefly and lightly, but the moon was splendid now. In her showy radiance and the gleam of headlights, the damp street was the silver of mackerel.

'I don't know when I've eaten so well,' Catherine said, sipping an espresso, and meant it. 'Or so much,' she added with an exaggerated groan.

'Celestina's a wonder.' And when the plump proprietress appeared then to refill their cups, he said in a stage whisper, 'I've asked her to run off and live in sin with me, but she says her husband would beat her.'

Celestina laughed and left them alone. By now the other diners were gone and the busboy was just cleaning the last table across the room, where a family had made a happy mess of their spaghetti.

They had kept the conversation throughout dinner on a casual and safe level. Now, the busboy having finished his chores and vanished discreetly behind the curtained doorway, they found themselves in sole possession of the dining room. A Christmas tree twinkled garishly in one corner. A candle sputtered in its straw-covered bottle.

Their conversation slowed and faltered.

Catherine leaned across the table, her eyes on his, and took his hand. 'Jack,' she began, and at the same moment he said, 'Catherine.'

They laughed, dispelling that brief moment of tension. 'You first,' Jack said with a smile.

'I've left Walter,' she blurted out, not at all the pretty speech she had rehearsed earlier. He lifted an eyebrow and waited for her to go on. 'For good,' she added. She fidgeted with her napkin and managed to drop it on the floor. Jack was up before she could reach it and handed it back to her. 'I'm such a nuisance,' she said.

'The most beautiful nuisance I've ever seen.'

She gave him a grateful smile, took a deep breath and began to talk; haltingly at first, and then in a rush that came spilling out faster than she could think. 'When I lost . . . when Becky died, the way she did, so horribly, it was like . . . I don't know exactly how to say this. I think — no, I *know* — that for a time I lost my mind, in the most literal sense. In a way, though, when I began to recover, I realized that it had opened me up to myself, to life, like I had never been before. All I could think about was all the time I hadn't spent with her, all the things that we hadn't done together, those things that you are always going to get around to, but never do. The words that never get said. And I saw how important these things might have been, and how unimportant were so many of the things I had done instead. How much of our time had been wasted, and how precious every moment can be. It was as if my life had been burned away, and all that was left were the things that really mattered, the truly important things: love, and people and connecting with them. That's hard. I'm having to learn, but I know that I must learn.'

Her eyes were down as she said this, fearing what she might see in his expression, but now she looked up again into his face. 'You are one of the things that matter. I don't know after all these years how you feel. But I had to tell you that I love you. I've always loved you. I never stopped.'

He needed a few seconds to collect his

wits. He didn't know what he had expected to hear from her, but despite the hopes that never left him, this wasn't it. 'Lord, you do choose your moments, don't you?' he said.

'I think this time the moment chose me,' she said.

He took her hand again. 'Catherine, you must know — surely you realize — that I've never stopped loving you either. You're so entwined in my heart, it would kill me to tear you out. I know. I tried for years.'

Tears glinted in her eyes. She tried to say something in reply and found the words simply wouldn't come

'The miracle,' he said, 'is discovering that you still love me.'

★   ★   ★

Back in the Porsche, he started up the powerful engine and looked over at her in the dashboard's glow. 'Are we in any hurry?'

'The night is ours,' she said, suddenly shy.

113

'Good.'

Instead of turning toward West Hollywood, he pulled onto the freeway headed north. She didn't question him as the myriad lights of the Valley swept by. An endless stream of cars surrounded them on either side, but inside the Porsche there was only the glow of the moment.

After a while, they left the freeway and began to climb the two-lane road that ran through Topanga Canyon. It twisted and turned this way and then that. He was a good driver and the car seemed to sense exactly what he expected of it.

They went higher into the mountains, then made their way downhill, the car like a graceful bird in its descent. They came around a wide bend and the ocean spread out below them, a seemingly endless black slate in the pale moonlight, marbled with ribbons of glittering foam.

He turned south on Pacific Coast Highway and she knew then where they were headed, and her heart began to beat a little faster with the knowledge.

★　★　★

It was all too obviously a man's apartment, everything dark and crowded, and had the look of one that had been lived in comfortably for years. A threadbare brown sofa and a much more comfortable-looking leather recliner with a reading lamp beside it, and a pile of books on a nearby table. Piles of books everywhere, in fact, and crowded shelves of them as well. A reading man's room. A workstation with a computer took up most of one wall, and through an open doorway she could see a corner of a rumpled bed.

'You couldn't have just moved in here,' she said.

'The last resident left pretty well most of it behind. A friend of Weitman's. He got an assignment in Berlin and took not much more than his clothes and a laptop. I just had to carry in a suitcase or two.'

She turned, surveying the room again, and finally brought her eyes back to where he still stood just inside the door.

'Catherine.' He took a cautious step in her direction and halted again. 'When you said you were divorcing Walter — is that a done deal?'

'There's no decree yet. I haven't even filed. But I won't be going back. I don't think, frankly, he even wants me back.'

The more fool him, Jack thought, and said aloud, 'Because I'm not much of a one for poaching on another man's territory.'

She had removed her wedding ring earlier, dropping it into her jewel box with a sense of finality, and she held out her hand now for him to see the white band of skin on her finger.

He hesitated for a moment longer. 'I see,' he said, and then, still sounding unsure of himself, 'The question, of course, is, what are we going to do now?'

'This,' she said simply, and crossed in three quick strides to where he was standing, threw her arms about him and, stretching slightly on tiptoe, kissed him.

★   ★   ★

In the bedroom, Catherine stretched lazily, enjoying the feeling of happy satiation so long absent in her life. She opened a closet door, looking for something more comfortable than her jeans and sweater, found a worn blue bathrobe, and put it on.

Jack came in from the bathroom. He took her in his arms again, holding her close and kissing her tenderly. 'I have something to ask you.'

'No one but Walter. And not for years with him,' she said.

'That wasn't the question. The question is, will you marry me?'

It was her turn to be surprised. 'You know, darling, today you don't have to marry the girl just because you slept with her.'

'But I do. I do have to marry you. It's what you were saying earlier: I don't want to waste any more time either. Say yes. You have to say yes.'

'Yes,' she said. 'But I suppose you have heard of something called bigamy?'

'As soon as you are free. The very moment the divorce is final.'

She hugged him tightly. 'Marriage license or no, from this day forward I am yours. I am your wife.'

Later, wrapped in his warm embrace, she slept again — and dreamed of evil, a blackness descending upon her like a cloud, enveloping her, taking the breath, the very life out of her.

She woke with a cry, sitting bolt upright in the bed. Instantly Jack sat up too, taking her in his arms. She clung to him, sobbing against his broad chest, struggling to get her heart to beat at its normal rate. Finally, the sobs stopped and her breathing slowed. 'Better?' he asked.

She sighed deeply. 'Thanks. I'm sorry I woke you.'

'If that was a bad dream, it must have been a lulu.'

'Jack, there's something I have to tell you,' she said.

'Something bad?'

She nodded. 'It's quite a bizarre story, I'm afraid.'

She started with the tunnel of light when she had been shot, told him of the incidents in which she had seemed to travel to other locations, and ended with her experience with little Debbie and her mother in the shopping mall. He listened without interruption, hearing her through to the end.

'The story is crazy, I'll admit that,' he said. 'But I have one good reason to believe you. No, make that two — the first one being that I know you are not given to making up stories.

'And the other reason?'

'I saw you. In my office, that day when you — what did you call it? — traveled to see me. Just for a second. I thought I was going crazy, but I came in and there you were; only I could look right through you, and I blinked and you were gone.' He paused thoughtfully. 'And next thing I knew, I was sitting by you at a concert.' He grinned suddenly and snapped his fingers. 'You little devil! That wasn't a coincidence at all, was it?'

She smiled sheepishly. 'All's fair in love and war, so they say.' She grew quickly serious again. 'Jack, there's something more. Just now, when I woke up so frightened — something like that happened to me in my office as well. I think that this man, Yellow Beard, is stalking me. I don't mean physically; I mean, on an astral level.'

'Catherine, of course you're frightened,' he said patiently. 'But the two of you, sharing the same unique gift, traveling back and forth to one another? That really does stretch the imagination. What just happened to you was a nightmare, plain and simple.'

'Maybe you're right,' she said after a moment. 'But even so, that still leaves the big question: what am I to do? I can't bear it. Sometimes at night, I hear them — Becky, those other children, crying. It frightens me, terrifies me, but I must find these men. I must stop them. Surely that was why I was given this gift. Surely I have been given a mission.'

'Maybe you've just given that mission to yourself. Look, okay, I buy this business of your traveling — I have to; I've seen it for myself. But that doesn't mean it's now your job to track these men down. That's a job for professionals.'

She was disappointed that he did not believe her. She felt so sure inside herself that she was right. How could she expect anyone else to understand that, though? She didn't understand it herself.

'All right, setting that aside — and I'm not saying I agree with you, there's still that whatever-you-want-to-call-it; that dream, that vision I had of Yellow Beard. You are willing to believe me — believe the astral travel business, anyway — and I am more grateful for that than you could imagine. But who else would? How could I go to Roby Chang and tell her about the changes in his appearance, without telling her I am seeing these men on an astral level?'

'There is such a thing as an anonymous tip. And I am a newsman, meaning my sources are protected.'

She considered for a moment, then nodded. 'Yes. I think that might work.' She had been too close to the problem to see such an obvious solution.

'Tomorrow. I'll call this Chang woman first thing.' Which would, he thought but did not say, neatly turn matters over to the professionals, where they belonged, and leave Catherine safely out of it.

In a shabby cottage miles away, Lester Paterson sat up in bed, immediately awake, eyes staring into the darkness.

He had seen them, two of them, going at it. The bitch, and a man with her. He knew the man, too, or thought he did. His face was familiar.

Who were they? Was he a threat too, or just someone she knew? Why did her face keep teasing him? Even now, he could see it just off at the edge of his mind.

Nearby, Colley snored loudly. What a pig! Paterson got out of bed and padded into the kitchen to get a beer from the refrigerator.

He thought briefly of the man he'd seen with her. He'd seen that face somewhere. Maybe a movie? He had one actor on the hook already, that little pansy O'Dell. Maybe a friend of his?

He went into the living room and switched on the television. A dark glow seemed to blossom from it and course through him, like he had been sent a message. Only, he couldn't read the message. It faded away from him as he tried to grab hold of it.

What he needed was to track down that bitch, and find her he would. He didn't know what was going on, but he knew she was bad for him, and what was bad for him had to be eliminated. He closed his eyes and called her image to mind. If he worked at it, he could almost be there wherever she was, like they were spirits together. If he could only figure out what was the bond between them.

He had to kill her, of course. She was a threat to him, in some way he couldn't define. There was something else, though, that nagged at him. He almost felt as if they were related, the two of them. They weren't of course. He'd only had one sister, and she was dead. Still, it felt as if there were some *thread* — he didn't know what other word to use — tying them to one another.

Where had all this come from?

8

Catherine called her attorney to begin the divorce proceedings, and rang Walter to tell him. If he felt any dismay, he kept it carefully under control.

'Whatever he needs me to sign,' he said. 'Have him give me a call.'

She and Jack did all the things that every other couple in love normally does in those initial weeks together. Of course, not every couple got to practice astral projection.

'We'll make a game of it, why don't we?' Jack said. 'You pop in whenever and wherever you like, and try to keep me from spotting you, and I'll do my damndest to catch you at it.'

At first, he always caught at least a glimpse of her. By Friday, however, in the privacy of her office with the door closed, she projected herself into his office and stood for several minutes waiting for any sign that he saw her. When it became clear that he did not, she decided to brush up on yet another skill. She stood behind him and stared hard at the back of his head, willing him to telephone her.

For a long while, it seemed that she would be unsuccessful. Then, abruptly, he turned from his word processor, cast a glance around the room without spotting her, and picked up the phone. She waited just long enough to see that he was dialing her number, and was back at her desk in time to take his call.

'Tell me you didn't see me,' she said when he came on the line.

'Just now? No, not a glimpse, you just popped into my head all of a sudden . . . oh. That was you, wasn't it? Hmm. I suppose it might be all right to know that you can drop by unseen whenever you wish, but it's kind of scary to think that a woman can just plant an idea in a man's head whenever she chooses.'

'Darling, women have been doing that since Eve looked up and saw a glimpse of red in an apple tree.'

★   ★   ★

Jack woke during the night to find her sitting up in bed, arms clasped about her knees. She came easily into his arms when he reached for her. 'Another bad dream?'

'Not as bad as before. But I could feel him looking for me. It's like he is searching through space, trying to pin me down. And I'm so afraid that sooner or later he's going to find me.'

He held her tight. He wanted to tell her he would protect her, but how did you protect someone from a phantasm? Particularly one that might only be in her mind. He chided himself for his disloyalty, but he could not rid himself of a suspicion that Catherine's phantoms were a means of consoling herself.

Of one thing, he was certain: there was something more at play here than mere vengeance; something he could not yet put a name to. Even when she had gone back to sleep, resting comfortably in his arms, he found himself staring up at the ceiling, trying to understand the unease that nagged at him.

On Saturday morning, Catherine took Jack with her to Becky's grave. He was the first person with whom she had shared that particular pilgrimage, something he seemed to understand tacitly and respect.

He stood patiently while she removed a few weeds and arranged fresh flowers around the headstone. When she was satisfied with the result, she rose and he put one arm around her to hold her close and gave her all the time she needed in silence.

She shivered suddenly, and looked over her shoulder with frightened eyes. There was nothing out of the ordinary to be seen: a funeral service just emptying from one of the chapels down the hill; mourners collecting in little puddles around shiny cars.

'Someone walking on my grave, I guess,' she said, and shivered again.

He had again that worrisome sense of some doom pending. 'The air's gotten cool,' he said, taking her arm and steering her toward the Porsche.

She hated the thought of hurrying away from Becky's grave, but a dark cloud seemed to have descended upon her. She glanced up at the sky, and was surprised to see that it was still clear and blue.

* * *

'But what are we doing here, Trash?' Colley asked, steering the van slowly up the winding drive of Forest Lawn Memorial Park. 'How are we going to find any kids in a cemetery?'

'I don't know. It's just something I felt. Pull over,' Paterson said, indicating a parking area next to a chapel. The doors of the chapel swung open as they parked and a group of mourners began to file out.

Paterson and Colley sat in silence, watching. A young girl appeared, grown men on either side of her. Father? Uncle? Brothers? She was pretty, as near as they could tell from the distance; thirteen, maybe fourteen, with that air peculiar to adolescent girls, veering from graceful to awkward and back again in the space of a heartbeat.

'We'd never get a hold of her and get out of here,' Colley said.

Paterson opened the glove box, revealing the gun inside. His fingers itched to pick it up. He had an urge to . . . he wasn't sure what. To start shooting. Somebody. Something. Why *were* they here? He had felt this hunch while they were on the freeway, and followed it blindly until it had led them into the cemetery; but now they were actually here, he had no clue what or who he was looking for.

He glanced around. There was nobody else to be seen: just the group from the chapel and up the hill there, a silver Porsche. As he looked, it began to move, disappearing around a curve of the driveway that would take it to the exit.

The mourners were getting into limousines and cars, a black-suited man directing traffic. The girl had disappeared. Colley was right: it would be suicide to try anything in this crowd, in broad daylight, and no quick way to escape.

Anyway, whatever instinct had guided him to this place had faded into nothing. That tingling sensation he sometimes got was gone.

He slammed the glove-box door shut. 'Let's go,' he said. 'There ain't anything here for us.'

But there had been. He was sure of it.

★   ★   ★

Without asking, Jack drove from Forest Lawn to San Marino, to the Huntington Museum, one of their favorite spots in the long-ago past. Today it was the gardens that drew them. The rain had fled, leaving a pale December sunshine, the air brisk and pleasant, the sky a Chamber of Commerce dream.

They took the arbour-covered walk that led to the Japanese Tea Garden. In spring, clouds of lavender wisteria blossoms would mass overhead, their scent driving bumble-bees and hummingbirds into a happy delirium; but for now the naked branches twisted and matted together like sticks dropped in some giant child's game.

At the end of the walk, wide steps led down to the postcard-perfect Tea Garden. Even in winter its little rolling hills were a vivid green. A stream, man-made to look perfectly natural, meandered through them and in its dark water jewel-colored Koi darted among lotus leaves. A high arch of a bridge in glossy scarlet crossed the stream — for show only; there was a less spectacular span for actual stream-crossing — and on the opposite bank a path led to the farthest hillside, where open shoji panels invited the eyes into a reproduction of a classical Japanese home.

Hand in hand, they followed the stream's path, laughing at the Koi who swam into the shallows of the bank and mouthed their pleas for food, mindless of the signs that forbade their feeding.

They stopped at the foot of the scarlet bridge, roped off to bar trespassers. Catherine eyed the perilously steep ascent. 'You have to wonder how the geishas got up and down them in their sandals, don't you,' she said. 'And they did it so gracefully. I think I should have to crawl.'

'Not exactly how one imagines Madame

Butterfly's entrance,' a voice said at her elbow.

She turned, and gasped. 'What are you . . . ?'

Roby Chang's penetrating glance swept over her and to Jack's puzzled expression, and back to Catherine again.

'We have to talk,' she said.

★   ★   ★

They met by arrangement at a Big Boy restaurant in Burbank, where they ordered breakfast before addressing the real reason for their meeting. They made small talk until the food came and the waitress had satisfied herself that these three wanted nothing more.

'Just a little privacy, if we may,' Chang said, with a smile that took any sting out of the remark. 'Now,' she said when the waitress had gone, 'Who's first?'

Catherine had already decided on her way there that she would tell Chang everything. She began to talk in a low voice that, Chang noted approvingly, wouldn't easily be heard at a neighboring table.

The everyday-ness of their surroundings made Catherine's recital all the more fantastic. She told of astral spirits that soared through space and fiends that skulked in shadows, while around them a dissonance of voices rose and fell and dishes clattered. The aroma of freshly baked bread wafted by them. At a nearby table a couple argued in sibilant whispers, and at another a trio of children squealed and laughed in carefree delight. A baby cried. Against this backdrop of the commonplace, the pages of Catherine's eerie story turned.

Chang ate as she listened without comment. She found herself thinking of the King. He would nail her to the cross on this one. Astral projections? Angels with messages? And a pair of killers, molesting a little girl in a dream.

Yet that much, at least, was not fantasy. Really, none of it appeared to be, however bizarre it sounded. At least, when Catherine Desmond talked of those two, her anger was real, her sincerity evident. Certainly she believed the story she was telling. This was no made-up fantasy hatched in a morbid mind still grieving for a lost child.

Catherine finished and sat waiting for the agent to respond.

'And that's all of it?' Chang pushed her cleared plate aside. 'I don't suppose you'd want to give me a demonstration of this . . . this gift of yours, would you?'

'It doesn't work quite like that. Physically I would still be here, sitting right where I am.'

'But your — what did you call it — your Ka, would be across town?'

'Yes, it's my Ka, my spirit, whatever you want to call it, that travels.'

'But she'd look like she had simply fallen asleep,' Jack said. 'And I have to tell you, I have seen her when she travels. She's appeared in my office a couple of times, when she wasn't physically there.'

'There is one thing I forgot to mention,' Catherine said. 'When they were with that little girl, I heard the one I call the Bear say 'trash can.' It was such an odd thing to say, wasn't it?'

'Trash can?' Chang's head came up, her eyes sharp on Catherine's face.

'Yes. Does that mean something?'

Chang smiled. At last something she could sink her teeth into. 'Trash Can Paterson,' she said. 'I've been wanting to catch up to that bastard.'

She motioned to the waitress for the check, and shook her head when Jack reached for his wallet. 'No, this is on the Bureau. At the least, my boss is going to find this fascinating. Let me talk to him.'

And maybe get myself tossed out of his office, and out of a good job, while I'm at it, she thought, but did not say aloud.

★　★　★

To her surprise, the King did not toss her out and did not laugh. He heard her through without a word and leaned so far back in his chair she thought it would surely overturn, his hands folded behind his head, eyes ceiling-ward, unlit cigarette dangling from the corner of his mouth. The silence was agonizingly long.

'You believe her?' he asked finally.

Chang took a deep breath. 'I do,' she said. 'I don't pretend to understand it,

135

but I really think she's telling us the truth. And Trash Can Paterson is no fantasy, certainly. He's slipped out of two seemingly certain convictions, and has been out of sight since then. And this sounds like his sort of doings.'

He continued to stare at the ceiling. She resisted an impulse to look up.

'Gabronski.' His chair came down with a thud and he looked straight and hard at her, the way he did when he had made up his mind about something. But what? she wondered. 'Never heard of him?'

'You mean *Doctor* Gabronski? The so-called L.A.P.D. psychic?'

'He's really not L.A.P.D., but he did help them with the Boulevard Strangler a couple of years back. Led them right to the scene of the crime, didn't he?'

'Yes, sure, that was the story at the time, though I have to admit I thought the media was hyping it up a bit. But isn't Gabronski, well . . . ' She faltered. 'Are you suggesting . . . well, do you think . . . ?' She picked her words carefully. 'Would the Bureau actually use somebody like him in a case?'

'Has used. And not somebody like him. Him. A couple of times, as a matter of fact.'

She was genuinely astonished. 'I didn't know. Never heard.'

He shrugged that off. 'It was all very low-key, no publicity. He didn't give us very much — a couple of leads, minor ones that helped a bit. It was kind of a draw for us. Which is why we never gave the story out.'

'And you're suggesting,' she said tentatively, because she didn't want to come out of this conversation looking like a complete idiot, 'maybe I should have him take a look at what we've got here?'

'It couldn't hurt anything, could it? This Gabronski might have some ideas we can use. And it's kind of down his alley, isn't it? Anyway, if we keep it quiet and it doesn't pan out, we're no worse off than we are now.'

9

'I thought you didn't believe in this stuff?' Jack said.

'I don't know personally if there's really anything to this guy or not,' Chang said. 'I'm just saying, he may be able to give us some advice.'

Catherine certainly hoped so. She was more convinced than ever that Paterson was stalking her on an astral level, but she knew that Jack was unconvinced. What was the point of arguing? Unless this Doctor Gabronski had something to offer, what on earth could anyone do about Paterson's stalking? If any help was to be forthcoming, it probably would not be of this earth, though she didn't understand that either.

Chang turned into a drive with an ivied gate and a sign reading 'Happy Acres.' A button on the gatepost produced a muffled voice. Chang identified herself and after a pause, the gate swung open and closed quickly behind them.

'A rest home?' Catherine asked.

'Hospital. Very private, very expensive.' The drive snaked past neatly manicured lawns to a massive faux Tudor house. Gravel crunched beneath their feet as they walked to the wide steps that led to a heavily carved wooden door.

A white-suited orderly, looking more like a football lineman than a nurse, opened the door a few inches, his thick body blocking the doorway. Chang flashed her badge. He stepped back without glancing at it and swung the door wider to let them in, and closed it carefully behind them, the lock snapping noisily into place.

'This way,' he said. He led them to a closed door, which he opened for them and stepped aside. 'Wait here,' he said, and left them. Again there was the snap of a lock as the door closed. Elegant or not, the hospital was certainly security-conscious.

They waited about five minutes before the door opened again and two men entered. The taller of them, rapier-thin, clean-shaven, came forward to shake hands. 'I'm Doctor Ederle. And this is

Doctor Gabronski,' he said, introducing his companion.

Doctor Gabronski was a tiny elfish man with long white sideburns and a beard that gave him a Santa Claus look, an effect enhanced by the little round belly that strained at a snugly closed vest of red, and the lively, intelligent eyes that sparkled through thick glasses. 'So very delighted you could come,' he said.

The introductions done, Doctor Ederle gave them a look that was not quite wary, but weighing. He glanced again at Gabronski, and made to go. 'I'll leave you to your chat. You'll call me, Doctor, if you need me?'

'Just so, thank you.' Doctor Gabronski's shiny bald pate bobbed up and down.

'I've had tea prepared,' Doctor Ederle addressed their visitors, 'and if you need anything else, or you have any difficulties, the bell is right there by the door.' He nodded briefly once more in Gabronski's direction and took leave of them.

Gabronski grinned and rubbed his hands together delightedly. 'Well, well,' he said. He gestured toward the waiting chairs and the highly polished tea service. 'Shall we have some tea?'

Catherine took tea, and Jack and Chang declined. They sat in a semi-circle near the fire. It was a cozy setting, and Catherine felt quickly at ease with their host, so that when he grew serious and prompted her with, 'Now then, I understand you have rather an unusual story. Suppose you tell it to me from the beginning,' she found herself repeating her strange tale without hesitation.

Gabronski listened attentively, only nodding his head occasionally to encourage her. When she had finished, he graciously refilled her cup and contemplated the fire for a brief moment. 'And you've come to me,' he said, his eyes going from face to face and settling on Chang's, 'to see if I can give you any insight into this — what did you say his name was — Paterson?'

'Well, yes, that too,' Chang said. 'But mostly, we wanted to see what you made of Mrs. Desmond's magic act.'

'Oh, not magic, certainly,' Catherine objected quickly. 'Though I'm not quite sure what to call it either. Doctor, you don't think I'm crazy, do you?'

His eyes twinkled. 'Crazy? No, absolutely not. But it is a singular story, isn't it? I don't think I've heard one like it before. Tell me, if you will, what do *you* think has happened? Is happening? You must have given it some thought.'

Catherine nodded. 'First of all, I think that I did die when I was shot, or very nearly died, at least. And I think I was sent back by someone — some*thing* — to try to stop these men. What I don't understand is, why me? I'm no kind of hero and I haven't any weapons to use against them. Even the astral projection, it doesn't accomplish much, does it? I mean, yes, I was able to interfere on one occasion, but there must surely have been others I didn't even witness. And when I am there, I have no physical presence. What I mean is, why was *I* picked for this? Why not a man, someone physically strong? Or a police person? Why not Agent Chang here?'

'Agent Chang would have had herself committed before this point,' Chang said, and added quickly, 'Sorry, Doctor, I don't mean to be flippant.'

'The point is, why did she choose me?' Catherine persisted.

'By 'she,'' Gabronski said, 'I take it you mean this individual who appeared to you first at the hospital and later, you think, in a flower shop.'

'It was a woman, both times. At least, she appeared as a woman. But I have sort of thought . . . well, do you think . . . might she be an angel?' She couldn't help feeling a little silly asking such a question, and she was aware that Chang stiffened slightly when she heard that word, but the doctor took it in stride.

'An angel?' He spread his hands. 'I couldn't say. That's a fairly modern concept, in any case, that of the smiling cherub. The Old Testament angels were warriors, mostly; quite fierce and not at all sweet. When Abraham's angel revealed itself, Abraham swooned in terror. And the cherubim were set outside Eden like a swarm of wasps to guard against Adam and Eve's returning. As for Lucifer, well, we need only recall that he was an angel himself before he fell from grace. Nothing cute about any of them. I shouldn't think your visitor was anything like those. But, spirit, yes; someone from beyond this existence, I think that's evident. Some-one, it would have to be, very concerned; someone who loved you very much on this plane and carried that love, that concern, through to the other side.'

Catherine took a sip of tea that had grown cold and thought about what he had said. 'A woman who — ' she started to say, but he interrupted her.

'Not necessarily. That's the point I was getting to. You are here before me at this moment, a woman, a young woman. If I may be permitted, a beautiful woman. But your soul is neither woman nor man, young nor old, beautiful nor ugly. Those are perceptions of our senses. We live in a physical world and it is our senses that make that world what we call 'real' to us. But this visitor is not a sensory reality; she is only an illusion projected to you by, as I say, someone who carried great love for you into the beyond, or someone with a powerful need to see these crimes redressed.'

He thought a moment. 'Is your mother alive?'

'Very much so,' she said with a smile.

'Father, then?'

'No, he passed away about ten years ago.' She had a sudden, bitingly vivid memory of her father sitting with her in a little boat on a summer afternoon, fishing without any great purpose, and telling her stories of his wartime adventures — mostly fictitious, as it turned out, but entertaining nonetheless. Yes, there had been a great love there, back and forth. She could see that he might well come from beyond to guide and protect.

She frowned. 'But if my father wished to come to me, to give me messages, help, why not simply project the image of himself?'

The doctor shrugged. 'Perhaps to make it easier for you to accept initially what he had to say. If your dead father had appeared to you, you would have been sure immediately you were hallucinating; you would have rejected out of hand whatever he had to say, attributed it to your injury, or the drugs you were being administered. That he was real, that his message was real, was probably the last thing you would have credited.

'But a woman . . . we tend to trust women more, I think, than we do men, logically or not. And a doctor . . . well, we put confidence in what a doctor tells us, don't we? If I were making a visit from the other side, and wanted you to take me seriously, I think I might very well have chosen the same appearance. Mind you, I can't know. I can only offer what seems to me an explanation.'

'All very interesting,' Chang said. 'But I can't see that this helps us any, other than your endorsement of Mrs. Desmond's experience. The question is, what do we do now? How do we make use of this . . . well, what would you call it — this gift she's been given? I'm not saying I buy it altogether; but if you're both right, then it had to have been given to her for a purpose, to use. But how?'

Gabronski studied Catherine carefully. 'I think I should like to see you do a projection.'

Catherine's throat went dry. 'If you feel

it will help,' she said. 'But I can't always do it at will. It sort of comes and goes.'

'I was thinking . . . ' He hesitated. 'I wonder if under hypnosis . . . if you would not object?'

'I'm not sure that's wise,' Jack said quickly. He did not voice what was really troubling him: if Cathcrinc's phantom stalker were really only a figment of her imagination, what might it wreak upon her in a hypnotic trance, the conscious mind and its protective capabilities lulled to sleep?

'You're concerned for her well-being, of course, as I am also. The advantage of hypnosis is, if there is any kind of threat to Mrs. Desmond, I can simply and immediately bring her back. Safer, I think, than what you have been doing. And there are some suggestions I can plant, for making this easier to do in the future, for instance. And most especially, for protecting herself.'

'In that case, yes,' Catherine said with determination, swallowing her anxiety. 'Let's do it.'

Jack bit his tongue. More and more he

felt as if he were on the sidelines in a game he little understood, with rules unknown to him. He sensed there was something not altogether innocent in Catherine's alleged connection to Paterson; a passion beyond what was altogether rational, something that instinct told him was dangerous.

Gabronski took a few minutes to set the stage. He closed heavy draperies over the windows and dimmed the already dim lights further, and brought a footstool for Catherine's feet. 'No need to lie down, the chair will be fine. So long as you're comfortable?' He lifted an eyebrow.

'Quite.'

'What about us?' Chang asked. 'Do we hold hands and concentrate, like at a séance? Or what?'

He smiled tolerantly. 'Just move your chairs back a bit — there, that's fine,' he said. 'And try to remain quiet, please.'

At the doctor's instructions, Catherine closed her eyes and began to breathe deeply. His voice was low and coaxing. She found herself going under easily, naturally, her tension fading.

'You will cloak yourself in the light,' his

murmuring voice told her. 'The light will protect you. And you will remain invisible to all eyes. You will be only a witness. You will see, and remain unseen, safe within the shielding light.'

She drew the light around herself as he instructed and felt its protective comfort invade her, relieving her anxieties. Her breathing deepened.

'In the future, you will do this yourself whenever you choose — easily, naturally . . . in the light . . . '

Help me, help me . . . The cries came from a great distance; not just Becky's voice, an entire chorus of young voices calling to her. *Help me . . . help . . . help . . .*

'Cloak yourself in the light . . . '

She slipped effortlessly downward — and found herself standing in a playground. In the distance, two young boys tossed a baseball back and forth; but closer to where she stood, the small carousel, the teeter-totter and the swings were all empty of children. There were only two men nearby, seated on a bench, watching the boys play, and . . . Her heart skipped a beat. The two men were Paterson and the Bear. For a moment she hung back, her fear resurfacing; and then she heard the doctor's voice within her and did as he instructed, reaching again for the light as if she had known all along how to do this, wrapping it once more about herself.

'Here he comes now,' the Bear said. They looked at her. No, she realized, *through* her, at someone approaching from behind. For a moment, though, she thought Paterson looked directly into her eyes.

She shrank away from him . . . and was back in the doctor's cozy room, the fire crackling beside her, that moment of terror like a scent lingering in her senses.

The sudden opening of her eyes gave Gabronski a shock. He had been in control, fully expecting to bring her back in due time on his instructions. It was rare, almost unheard of for a subject to awaken on her own. That, more than anything else, told him how frightened this woman really was, far more frightened than she had admitted or shown. He ought to have realized that, he scolded himself.

'You are fine, you are safe,' he told her quickly, and reached to take one of her hands in his. It was ice-cold.

'*Are* you okay?' Jack demanded, kneeling by her chair and turning her face toward him.

'Yes. I . . . ' She hesitated, still disoriented, trying to collect her thoughts. 'It was *them:* Paterson and the Bear. They were in a park, a children's playground, watching two little boys play, and waiting for someone. The Bear said 'here he comes,' and then I woke up back here.'

'Did they see you?' Gabronski asked, still distressed and puzzled by her sudden awakening.

'I . . . I don't know. I thought not, but then Paterson looked at me, as if he were looking into my eyes. It . . . it startled me. I'm sorry. I panicked. That's what brought me back.'

'That third person you said you sensed,' Chang said in an excited voice, 'did you see who he was?'

Catherine shook her head. 'No. He was approaching from behind me. They looked toward him; looked through me, I thought. Only, as I said, Paterson might have glimpsed me, or maybe he only sensed me. He seems to do that.'

Chang jumped up from her chair, clenching her fists. 'We need to know who they were meeting.'

'I'll go back,' Catherine said, but her voice was tremulous, without conviction.

'No. You can't,' Jack said firmly. He understood how Chang and Gabronski felt, but Catherine's safety was his first concern. 'Look at her, she's white as a ghost. I'm not going to let her go there again.'

Catherine started to reply, but Gabronski gave his head a vehement shake. 'I think he may be right,' he said. 'There's something else. I've been thinking about this, and I don't like it. You say that this person has only recently begun to, as you put it, stalk you? And that he has quickly grown stronger at it, his presence more real with each occasion?'

'Yes. At first it was only a vague feeling, but each time it gets worse. Even now, wrapped in the light as you instructed me, I had this sense that he knew I was

152

there; that he could step right up to me, take me in a stranglehold . . . ' She gasped with the memory and buried her face in her hands. 'It's horrible. I can't describe it.'

Gabronski nodded. He at least seemed to have quite accepted Catherine's stalker as real. After a moment, Jack asked, 'If it is true, if he really is stalking her on some invisible level, what can we do about it?'

Gabronski's earlier jolly demeanor was gone entirely. He frowned while he considered the question. At length he said: 'I have an idea that perhaps this individual, this Paterson . . . that perhaps he too has psychic abilities, abilities that may even have been heretofore untapped. He might have been totally unaware of them until recently, though probably he used them from time to time without thinking about it, or maybe he simply considered them hunches. Many people have these gifts — even use them, without being consciously aware of them.' He looked directly into Catherine's face. 'But there is some powerful link between the two of you on the astral plane. I very much fear that your visits to him may have been what awakened whatever gifts he possesses, may even be feeding them.'

'You mean every time I see him I am making him stronger, leading him to me?'

'It would appear so. I think to visit this individual again may be to place yourself in grave danger.'

'But I can't stop, don't you see?' Catherine said in a plaintive voice. 'If this is what I was sent back for, I have to see it through.'

'Catherine, you don't even know that you were 'sent back' for any purpose,' Jack said angrily. 'At best that's just a guess on your part. And for what purpose? You said these voices told you there was something only you could do. How could that mean catching these two monsters? That's what the police are for, isn't it? People like Chang, here. How can you imagine that you're the one, the only one, who could do that?'

'I don't know,' she admitted with a shrug. 'I only know I have no choice but to continue down this road.' Her voice dropped to a near-whisper. 'This life that

I was given back — it isn't really mine to own, is it? It was only lent to me, as I see it. And maybe that's the point: that I was killed, and the very worst that could happen to me is that I'll end up back where I was when Paterson shot me.'

Jack wanted to say 'that's the very worst thing that could happen to me, too,' but her eyes pleaded with him for understanding. Understanding that he did not have to give. He swallowed his frustration and said nothing.

'Anyway,' she said into his silence, 'whether I was given some heavenly mission or not, now that I know who and what he is, I can never rest until I see him brought to justice. I owe Becky that. I owe it to all those weeping children.'

Chang shot Gabronski a quick look, but he only shook his head sadly. 'Yes, I can understand that,' he said softly. He folded his hands across his belly. 'It's intriguing, isn't it? You speak of an angel, but really, doesn't it seem that you have two angels — the bright one, and a dark one? You are wed to both of them, I think, for reasons that we cannot yet perceive.'

'Is there no way to protect myself from that dark angel?' Catherine asked.

He sighed. 'Only the light. It was the light, your bright angel, who sent you on this mission. We have to believe she will protect you. Of one thing I am certain. I know evil of this magnitude; I have experienced it before — and nothing on this mortal plane could protect you from it. There are no crosses, no silver bullets, no wooden stakes to kill such demons when they are within you.'

★　★　★

They were quiet on the way back to Los Angeles. After a time, to relieve the somber mood, Jack said, 'A charming man, that Gabronski.'

'Yes,' Catherine agreed with him, glad to be diverted from her morbid thoughts of Paterson. 'Is he the chief of the hospital?'

'That's Ederle,' Chang said. 'He's the chief. He runs Happy Acres.'

'In any case, the patients must adore Doctor Gabronski.'

'Doctor Gabronski is a patient at Happy Acres,' Chang said. In the wake of their astonished silence, she negotiated her way past a slow-moving Toyota.

'A patient?' Catherine finally managed to ask. 'Not a doctor?'

'He's a doctor, yes — or at least he was.' She changed lanes with a blast of her horn and focused for a few seconds on the heavy freeway traffic.

'You're both too young to remember, of course,' she said after a moment. 'I don't personally remember it myself. It happened thirty or more years ago, but it's something of a Bureau legend. Gabronski murdered a string of children. Five, I think, before he turned himself in. Claimed he'd been possessed by a demon. They found him insane, naturally. He's lived at Happy Acres ever since. It's a mental hospital, a very discreet one. He's a model patient, they tell me.'

10

Chang dropped them at Catherine's apartment. On an impulse, Jack suggested a drive to Laguna Beach. 'You need to get away from everything,' he said. 'Forget all this business for one evening, at least.'

The suggestion was a good one. The weather had turned warm, as it could do in the California winter; and off-season, Laguna was mostly empty of the tourists that in summer packed its sidewalks and restaurants. Except for an occasional roller-skater, they had the Promenade that snaked along the beachfront to themselves. The turquoise water deepened to blue-black where it stretched toward the hump of Santa Catalina Island just visible on the misty horizon.

Closer, the surf washed in rivulets over the sand and formed little tidal pools in the rocks that dotted the shore below the ragged bluffs. They scrambled over the rocks and examined the miniature aquariums with their brilliant anemones, purple urchins, huge sea slugs and skittish crabs.

The daylight faded and they abandoned the slippery rocks. They had dinner at Dizz's As Is, an intimate shingled house whose walls sported a photo gallery of the in-crowd of Hollywood's glamour heyday. Judy Garland, Clark Gable, Lana Turner and myriad others smiled their approval down on the vermouths they sipped and the rack of lamb that followed. As if by common agreement they spoke not at all of Gabronski or Chang or Trash Can Paterson. Jack was happy to see that by the time Catherine was sipping an espresso, her face had lost that haunted look she had worn for the last several days.

It was late by the time they settled into the Porsche again and headed north on the San Diego Freeway, a lustrous pewter moon winking off and on through patches of cloud overhead. Catherine leaned against the soft leather upholstery, one hand in Jack's, and savored the feeling of deep relaxation. Somewhere between Los

Angeles International Airport and Santa Monica Boulevard, relaxation became sleep.

Glancing over at her in the dashboard's pale luminance, Jack felt himself engulfed in a tide of emotions: love, concern, protectiveness. Her suggestion that life had only been lent to her this time around for one specific purpose, and one purpose only, would not bear his contemplating. He was sure that, if she really had been 'sent back,' it was as much to share life with him as to ferret out a pair of admittedly evil child molesters.

He still thought that her belief that she had been given a mission might be nothing more than self-delusion, fed by her desire to avenge her daughter's death. One thing that he had come to realize: if Paterson was stalking her, as she believed, Catherine was stalking him, as well. In some bizarre psychic way, they were each of them feeding a need in the other.

Anyway, hadn't she told him that she had heard him call to her when she was hovering between life and death? That clinched it as far as he was concerned; and though she might think it treasonous, he was determined that their love for one another would take precedence over anything else, Paterson included.

So, as he backed the car into a parking place near Catherine's apartment, it was with no great happiness that he saw Chang's now-familiar red Bronco parked just outside the front door.

She was waiting for them on the sidewalk as they walked up. 'Chang,' he said before either of the women could speak, 'I know how important this case is to you, but you've got to see that this is tearing Catherine apart.'

'Yes, you're right,' Chang said with a sigh. 'I know that. Only ... ' She hesitated.

'Only?' Catherine prompted, already sure what she was going to hear.

'There's been another one. A boy this time, snatched from a playground. I suspect the very playground where you saw them earlier today.'

Catherine fumbled in her purse for her keys. 'Come up. I'll make coffee.'

They sipped coffee in Catherine's living room while Chang gave them the details. They could faintly hear the hum and clang of Santa Monica's traffic even through the closed balcony door. A fire on the grate offered a welcome respite from the cool December air.

The discussion grew heated as well. For all the dread that it bred within her, Catherine felt more strongly than ever that she had to find Paterson and his companion before they did more of their evil. Perhaps if she had after all gone back to that playground a second time when she was with Gabronski, she might have found some way to prevent this latest kidnapping. That was a suggestion, however, with which Jack strongly disagreed.

'It's too dangerous for you,' he insisted.

Chang was torn. She cared about Catherine; cared about both of them. Jack was right, of course: it was dangerous. She understood how he felt. Probably, in his shoes, she would feel the same way.

The bottom line remained the same for her, however. She had some bad guys to catch, really bad guys. And so far,

Catherine was her best shot — hell, her only shot — at catching them.

'But it doesn't have to be dangerous, does it?' she argued, wanting to convince herself as well as them. 'Gabronski talked about wrapping yourself in the light, so they don't see you. It's that simple, isn't it? You hide yourself in the heavenly glow, you find them, you go outside . . . You can go outside, can't you?'

'I don't know,' Catherine said thoughtfully. 'I wouldn't be able to turn a door knob; that requires some physicality, and I haven't mastered that yet. But since I have no body, I suppose I could just pass through a door. I've never tried.'

'Well, then, that's what we need. If you can go outside, you can get me an address. A house number, a street name. Anything. That's all. Then you come home. You won't have to put yourself at any kind of risk.'

'Won't she?' Jack said. His stomach churned at the very idea. 'Gabronski also told us he thought every time she visited Paterson she was making him stronger, bringing him closer to finding her.'

Catherine sighed. 'Don't worry, darling, I will be careful. I'll do what Chang says — pop in just long enough to see them, and back out again. And I do think I can manage to remain unseen. Maybe if he doesn't see me, he won't know that I'm there.'

Jack remained unconvinced, but he already knew the futility of arguing. He swallowed his frustration. 'Can you just do this now at will?' he asked instead.

She shrugged. 'I can try. Gabronski gave me that suggestion when he put me under earlier, didn't he? It's as good a time to find out as any.'

She slipped off her shoes and stretched out on the sofa, plumping up a pillow for her head. Jack sat on the floor by the sofa. Chang got up to dim the lights. By the time she sat down again in her chair, Catherine's eyes were already closed, her breathing slow and deep.

★   ★   ★

'It's a thousand bucks,' Paterson said, and when the man seated opposite him hesitated, he added quickly, 'It's the best one yet, worth every penny, I promise you. This kid's cute as a bug. You can watch some of it if you want to.'

'No, that's okay, you're cool.' Danny O'Dell took out his wallet and peeled off ten one-hundred-dollar bills, laying them neatly on the filthy tabletop. The place was a pigpen, he thought. It even smelled like one. He wrinkled his fastidious nose. Well, what could he expect? When you lay down with dogs . . .

Paterson did not so much as glance at the money. 'You hear that, Colley? We are coo-ol.' He made two syllables of it. 'Cool, I like that. Have another line, bro.' He indicated the cracked mirror on the tabletop with its mound of cocaine. 'Colley, get our friend a beer.'

'No thanks, I have to go.' O'Dell slipped the DVD into an inside pocket of his jacket and jiggled his keys as if to leave, but he lingered for a moment.

'Do you . . . ' he started to ask, and paused hesitantly, before he screwed up his courage to ask the question that had puzzled him for some time. 'Do you guys ever feel bad? You know, guilty about any of this?'

Paterson's look was at once amused and darkened underneath like clouds before a storm. 'Guilty?' he echoed. 'What are you talking about, guilty? You some kind of Puritan, are you, thinks sex is evil? I notice you're quick enough to run here when I tell you I've got a new movie for you. Are *you* feeling guilty?'

The actor showed a trace of embarrassment. 'No, you're probably right,' he said. He looked away from Paterson's ferocious glower.

'Course I am. Say, you want to try some for yourself? The real stuff, I mean, not just movies of it. We can set that up for you, too, you know.'

O'Dell swallowed. He didn't really like talking about this sort of thing. Watching it, yes; imagining it . . . but until Paterson, he had never actually confessed his special interests to anyone. How had Paterson wormed it out of him, anyway? He didn't actually remember. They had been doing drugs, drinking. Somehow they ended up watching a movie, one of the special ones. Paterson had reeled him in like a fish on a line.

'How about I fix you up with the next one?' Paterson said, so offhanded, he might have been discussing a deal on a used car. 'Cost you, say, five thousand.'

For a moment O'Dell actually considered the offer. The money didn't deter him. He could afford that. It was the idea that frightened him, though. It even sickened him a little when, as now, he considered it.

He knew himself well enough, though, to know that he would feel no such shame when he arrived home and immediately put the new DVD into his player, locked his bedroom door, and watched it through to its end. Then, he would be filled with fantasies of the very thing Paterson was offering to arrange for him, and would berate himself as a fool for not taking up the offer.

Now, though, with these two watching like a pair of vipers getting ready to strike, he hadn't the courage to say yes. 'I'd better not,' he said with a roll of his eyes that would have been entirely familiar to his television audience. 'Too risky. What if I was recognized?'

'We can put a mask on you. I don't guess anyone would recognize your pecker, would they? That's not famous, is it?'

Paterson laughed again, but suddenly his eyes narrowed and he shot a look around the room as if someone had entered it, peering into every corner.

'What is it, Trash?' Colley glanced around too, puzzled and concerned at the same time.

Paterson's sudden look of alarm spooked O'Dell. 'Did you hear something?' he asked, genuinely frightened. Just being found here, with the drugs and the movies, would ruin his career. Nobody was going to sponsor a children's television show hosted by an actor arrested for drugs and kiddie porn.

I must be crazy coming here, he thought. In the future, he would make arrangements to meet somewhere. Or maybe there shouldn't be a future. He had half a dozen movies, surely he didn't need more. What more was there to see?

Except — a new face, a different body. A new fantasy. That was what it was, yes. He lived in a world of fantasies; they were his stock in trade. That was what excited him, not the reality. He would never really do what Paterson suggested. That was sick. He only wanted to watch, not even in the flesh, but at a remove, on his television screen. That was the difference between him and them.

Paterson shook his head and looked calmer, but there was an underlying anxiety that didn't quite leave his eyes. 'Nah. I just like keeping an ear tuned, is all.'

'I'd better go.' This time O'Dell did get up, a little too quickly. He patted the pocket with the DVD in it, slipped his hat on his head and the dark glasses over his eyes. 'I'll let myself out.'

When the door had closed behind him, Paterson strode quickly across to lock it. 'I'll let myself out,' he mimicked in a falsetto voice. 'Pansy.'

Colley took a long sip of his beer. 'You know, Trash,' he said, speaking slowly, 'There was one of those kids at least didn't have any fun.'

Paterson wheeled on him. 'What are you talking about? You bringing that up again?' He grabbed an ashtray off a table and flung it at Colley, ashes and cigarette butts leaving a trail across the dirty carpet. The glass ashtray caught Colley on the shoulder.

'Ouch! Damn it, Trash, that hurt.'

'Don't you be throwing that business up to me,' Paterson railed at him. 'You know damn well it wasn't my fault what happened.'

Colley wilted in the face of his harangue. 'You're right, Trash.' He rubbed his bruised arm meekly.

'Listen, you don't like what we're doing, you just take your butt out that door. You go on and quit right this minute. Maybe the prissy little TV host will give you a job.'

'I didn't say I wanted to quit, Trash.' Colley's voice had become a whine.

''Cause there's plenty of guys would like to be getting what you're getting and get paid for it too,' Paterson said, pacing back and forth in long, quick strides.

170

'Hell, I know that. I wasn't complaining.'

'Well, don't you be. And don't you be talking about her; it wasn't my fault. Damn, that makes me sore.'

'I'm sorry, Trash. I didn't mean nothing. I was just running my mouth, you know what I'm like. I'm not as smart as you.'

'You got that right,' Paterson said more calmly, mollified. 'And don't you forget it either.'

Colley clamped his lips tightly together and turned on the TV news. Paterson was about to tell him to turn the damned thing off when he remembered something: a man on the television screen. Not this man, but another one, working his yap about something, the Middle East maybe, blah, blah, blah.

TV! That was it. That was where he had seen the bitch's boyfriend, the man he had seen in the sack with her. He was some kind of news reporter.

He sat down in a chair in front of the screen, staring at it, hardly even noticing what he saw. He knew who *she* was, too.

171

Catherine Desmond. Why hadn't he tumbled onto it sooner? And she had been here, just minutes ago. Maybe not in the flesh, but her ghost, her something. He was sure of it.

★   ★   ★

Going through the door had been easy after all, the wood no more substantial to her than a wisp of a cloud. Outside, Catherine looked back at the house she had just left, a fake New England cottage that years ago had probably been charming. Once-white paint was now dingy and peeling, dark green shutters hung askew. A curdle of shrubs, over-grown and badly in need of a trim, lined the walk; and a bamboo fence, eight feet high, blocked the view from the street. A rusty van and an Oldsmobile of question-able vintage sat in the drive, both license plates splattered with mud so that all but one or two of the numbers were illegible.

Chang needed an address. The house numbers too had been disguised, but the paint that had been daubed over them

had not quite covered them. Three seventeen, she thought, or maybe fourteen. All
she needed, then, was a street name.

Moving along the drive was oddly like
walking. She could almost feel her steps
making contact with the cement, though
she knew that wasn't possible. Or was she
gaining physicality?

No sidewalks here, only a narrow strip
of weedy grass. A rusty mailbox tilted
starboard on a bare wooden post. She
reached for the mailbox door, thinking
there might be letters inside, but her hand
went right through the metal latch. So
much for physicality.

She heard the familiar growl of a car's
engine and the whine of tires going fast
on pavement. The headlights of a car shot
past an intersection maybe fifty yards
away.

Of course, even in the country, even
where people made it clear they wanted
to be left alone, streets and roads were
marked, weren't they? She moved in that
direction and found it easy to hurry;
found, in fact, that she could move as fast
as she wished, virtually flying.

Yes, there was a street sign: Morning View Road. And the cross street . . . she came closer to the sign, and found the scene before her fading rapidly, growing paler. She paused and took a step back. Her sight grew slightly clearer.

She thought about that for a moment. It was Paterson to whom she traveled, to whom she was linked, and apparently she could only travel so far away from him before the link began to weaken.

She tried again to get close enough to read the next sign. She made out a letter A. Au. Or was it Av? Yes, Av, Avalon, she was sure of it, but when she moved closer still, wanting to confirm, it faded into oblivion, and she felt the solidity of her sofa beneath her. She was back in her apartment, Jack leaning over her anxiously, Chang watching from her chair.

'Are you all right?' Jack asked.

'Yes,' she said after a moment of mental inventory. 'Yes, I'm fine.' She even managed a smile. 'And they didn't see me, I'm sure,' she added. It had been a relief to find that she could indeed conceal herself from Paterson. She need not be so frightened of him, then, surely. 'And, I saw our 'third person' at last. Danny O'Dell, he was there with them.'

'The children's show, the little twerpy guy with the checked suits?' Chang said. 'Hell, that is disgusting, isn't it? Are you sure he was into this kiddie stuff with them? There could be all kinds of reasons why he was there. Maybe he sells Tupperware on the side.'

'No, he was buying a movie,' Catherine said. 'Paterson talked about the kid on it, a little boy, and O'Dell paid him a thousand dollars.'

Chang whistled. 'A thousand bucks. For sure that was no travel video. Jeez, that's a great lead. I can have this O'Dell creep put under surveillance. If he's actively into this filth, we'll get him.'

'There's more, too,' Catherine added triumphantly. 'I heard Paterson call his friend — the one I called the Bear — he called him Collie. Like the dog.'

Chang made a note. 'If he's got any kind of record, we can find him in the computer. What about an address? Did you get that?'

'Three seventeen, or it might have been three fourteen, Morning View Road, cross street, Avalon, I think. It's the first house down Morning View, maybe a quarter of a mile. And it's out in the country, very rural, a large open field across the way, no houses close around that I could see.'

'That should do it,' Chang said, but there was an odd hesitation in her manner.

Jack sensed it. 'That's enough for a warrant, surely, isn't it?' he asked.

Chang was thinking that maybe she was going too fast, asking for a warrant with nothing more to support it than Catherine's astral visit. She was still having a hard time getting her teeth into this ghost business. And the King wanted something concrete, not just visions.

On the other hand, they couldn't take a chance on Paterson slipping out of their hands, could they?

'I'll see my boss tomorrow,' she said aloud, 'and ask for the warrant.'

11

Jack found himself staring at the two images of Trash Can Paterson on his computer screen, trying to read the expression in the eyes of what were, after all, only an artist's renderings. It was almost as if Paterson had branded her with that bullet, he thought; marked her as his own. The two of them were linked, maybe, as Catherine believed, on some supernatural level.

He thought, not for the first time, that what he was fighting was not Paterson, but something within Catherine herself; something more than just the need to avenge her daughter. The two of them, she and Paterson, were on a collision course, racing toward one another with an equal and frightening determination.

When the collision finally came, what then?

★ ★ ★

It was a win some, lose some sort of case, as Chang saw it. The King agreed to the search warrant for the Morning View house, not without some reluctance.

'She saw this in a dream, right?' he asked and gave her a cautious look. 'You know, don't you, if this turns out to be a fiasco, we're going to have a lot of egg on our faces.'

'In an astral projection, yes,' Chang said, and added, 'I believe her, sir.'

'Well, let's go with it,' he said with a resigned sigh. 'We should have the warrant this afternoon, this evening at the latest. Assemble a team. Take all the guys you want. We don't want anybody getting away over a back fence. You'll have to include the L.A.P.D. — this Sergeant Conners, obviously. And the locals. It's county, right? Sheriff's deputies, then.'

For a moment she came close to urging him to move the warrant along; try to get it right away. Already time had passed since Catherine paid them her astral visit during the night. If Paterson had any inkling . . . But she dismissed her impatience as needless stewing. Paterson had no clue. Catherine was convinced of that. There was no reason to worry about his slipping out on them.

'What about this Danny O'Dell?' she asked instead. 'What about a warrant to search his place? Desmond says she saw him with Paterson.'

'Another of Mrs. Desmond's visions?' He snorted. 'Could be imagination. Could be indigestion. The guy's a TV star. My kids watch him. I don't want them kicking my butt because I made a false bust on their idol.'

* * *

Paterson's pictures hit the noon news. Chang was eating a sandwich at a favorite bar when she saw it, and nearly choked. Mere seconds later, her cell phone rang. She needed no special intuition to tell her it was the King.

'Damn and hellfire,' the King swore when she entered his office less than twenty minutes later. 'How did this happen?'

'Reporters,' was all Chang could say.

'Someone got nosey. I'll look around, but it may be hard to pin down. Desmond let something slip, maybe, or the boyfriend.'

'So what's your read on this?'

'It might spook him,' Chang said dejectedly. 'He could run.'

He thought about that. 'But would he? You get your picture on the TV, would you run, or hide? This place of his, you said it was totally isolated? No neighbors anywhere close?'

'Yes,' Chang agreed reluctantly.

He lifted an eyebrow. 'Well, there's no way he could know we've tumbled to his hiding place, right? Desmond was sure they didn't see her, you said.'

'Yes, she was sure, but . . . '

'But?'

'No, he doesn't know we know where he is.' She really hoped that was true.

★   ★   ★

It took them less than an hour to strip the place. 'Get everything in the van,' Paterson ordered the minute he saw his face on the television screen. 'And make

180

it quick. We got to get out of here.'

'Probably nobody around here even saw you,' Colley said, already loading up his arms with their possessions. 'You almost never go out in the daytime, and when you do you're in the van or that Olds you stole. And I go to the store for us. Anyways, there ain't nobody nearer to us than half a mile or more. Who'd see you? And there's no way anybody would find this place unless somebody did spot you. Hell, we're in the middle of nowhere.'

'Someone might've seen me, and I ain't waiting around here to find out. Besides, she knows where I am. I'd bet money on it. She was here, I knew it, damned bitch. I can just about smell her. Cops could be on their way here this minute. Put all them DVDs in a box; we ain't leaving them behind, not after what we did to make them.'

He immediately dialed a number. 'I need to talk to O'Dell. Tell him it's his friend Mike. Tell him it's important.' He fidgeted while he waited. That damn pansy had better not try to put him off.

He was in no mood.

'You aren't supposed to call here,' O'Dell said in a peeved voice.

'Yeah, well your cell phone was turned off or something. Listen, I need some money — five, six thousand at least. And that place of yours up in the mountains, I got to borrow it for a while.'

'That's not a good idea. A friend of mine was going to use it next weekend. Besides . . . '

'I don't give a rat's ass about any besides, or any friend of yours either. You can put them off somehow. I'm telling you I need it; I got to save my ass, and yours too, you dumb punk. This is serious!'

* * *

'You cleaned the prints off everything at the house?' Paterson asked for the fourth time.

'Course I did,' Colley said. A thought flashed through his mind: had he remembered the empty beer bottles on the kitchen counter? They had been in such a hurry. He thought he had. He squinted, trying to remember. He'd done the bedroom — he was sure of that — and the living room, and he remembered wiping off the stove and refrigerator. *I must have done the bottles*, he told himself.

They rocketed onto the 14 Freeway at high speed, the van careening briefly. Colley drove. Paterson was thinking about Catherine Desmond; about the way she seemed to pop in wherever he was.

How the hell does she do that? he wondered. He closed his eyes, seeing her in his mind . . .

★   ★   ★

They were at Catherine's apartment. Jack was kneeling, just laying a fire in the fireplace. And, out of nowhere, Paterson was there, standing just in front of her, grinning wickedly.

'Jesus,' Jack swore, rocking back on his heels. Catherine dropped a platter, scarcely aware of the crash or the broken crockery that scattered at her feet.

'You bastard,' Jack said. He grabbed up a log and leaped to his feet, swinging it at

183

Paterson — and it went right through him.

He's only a projection, Catherine thought. *He's no more physical than I am when I project. I have only to break his concentration . . .*

She lunged at him, hands up as if to ward off a blow; and as quickly, as easily as that, he was gone. But she had forgotten to avoid his eyes. They locked on hers even as she moved, and it was like a bullet exploding in her head all over again. She cried aloud in pain, and fell in a heap to the floor.

★   ★   ★

Paterson and Collie were gone. 'Bloody hell!' Chang swore aloud. Even without a search, she could see they had fled. Drawers were yanked out and upended, contents scattered on the floor, empty closets left open, shelves stripped bare: all the evidence of a hasty flight.

Somehow, Paterson had known. Spooked by the likeness on TV? Picked it up from Desmond's wavelengths? Maybe there was something to this psychic business. She looked around for anything that might salvage the day.

'They didn't waste much energy on decorating,' Conners said in a despondent voice.

'Or cleaning.' The place smelled of sweat and urine and rotting food. A ratty sofa, a couple of chairs, linoleum floors with most of the pattern worn off.

★   ★   ★

On the side of caution, Chang moved Catherine and Jack into a safe house, a little cottage on a side street in Hollywood, inconspicuous and obviously chosen with safety in mind. There were grates over the windows, and the front door had been wired with motion sensors that would provide early notice of any approach.

Chang went in first, pulling heavy draperies closed before she turned on the light, and gave the four rooms — living room, kitchen, bedroom, bath — a quick but sharp once-over. Satisfied, she motioned them in.

The interior was spartan but adequate: in the living room a television, a faded green corduroy sofa and a matching chair; an antiquated gas stove in the kitchen, as well as a dripping faucet that had left a permanent rust stain in the sink; but everything was clean, and the bed in the bedroom was surprisingly comfortable when Jack tested it.

'I've slept in worse,' he said.

'Home sweet home,' Catherine said wryly.

'I'll sleep outside for the night,' Chang said, 'in the Bronco. Just to be sure.'

'Wouldn't you be more comfortable on the sofa?' Catherine asked.

Chang gave the sofa a dubious look. 'On that thing? Never fear, I've slept in the Bronco plenty. Anyway, I don't want to wait till someone's standing by the sofa with a gun at my head before I know they're coming. Always get them before they get inside if you can.'

They had stopped on the way to pick up a pizza and some Cokes. They ate in a dispirited silence, watching the evening news with Paterson's picture now on every channel, and the story of the unsuccessful raid on the house in Canyon Country.

The pizza tasted like cardboard. Jack managed only a few bites before it stuck in his throat. Catherine had no more appetite than he did, but Chang finished her portion, drained the last of the Coke from her glass, and left them getting ready for bed. She was careful to be sure the door locked securely behind her. Like that was going to do any good, she thought, people passing through walls the way they did. She had never had to deal with anything like this before.

She settled into the Bronco and put her coat over her for a blanket. The rain had stopped and a pale moon cast a watery light. She slid the seat back as far as it would go, tried to find a comfortable position, gave up finally and sat upright, wishing she had a beer.

She had goofed. She had let Paterson and Colley get away. She should have known his picture on TV would send him running.

But had it? The King was right: the

smart thing would have been for him to stay put where he was. He couldn't know they had found his hideout. Running around in public with your face plastered all over TV wasn't the sensible thing to do. And she had a notion that this guy was smart enough all right, animal cunning at least. Protective cunning.

It hadn't looked like they had been gone from Morning View more than a little while. One of the beer bottles had still been on the cool side. That cigarette in the ashtray wasn't altogether out either; it had been smoldering for a bit. If she had gotten there just a little faster . . . Why hadn't she pushed the King for the warrant; moved the bust up even an hour or two?

She didn't like the answer that came to her.

★　★　★

Mommy, Mommy, help me . . . Catherine woke in terror, sweat-drenched, heart pounding.

She slipped quietly from the bed and

went to the living room. Despite the risk she knew she was taking, she sat on the sofa, closed her eyes, and willed herself into space.

At first she thought she had failed to find him. Then she saw him a short distance away — or barely saw him; the image was far fainter than anything she had seen before, fading in and out like a bad phone connection. A dark, shadowy location, no city lights, no neon, only the faintest moonlight.

She looked around, trying to find some physical clues, but the scene faded altogether and she was back in the living room of the little cottage, Chang watching her from the doorway.

'I saw the light go on,' Chang said. 'Just checking. You okay?'

'I tried to find him, but wherever he is, it's a long way from here. I saw a dirt street and a house; a shack, really. Not much more than that.'

'Mexico, maybe Tijuana,' Chang said. 'Which makes sense. If you're on the lam, that's a good bet. You can always pay off the locals there, if you've got the bucks.

189

What it tells me is that you're not in any immediate danger. It's a good two to three hours from here to the border. You can sleep without worrying.'

12

Catherine and Jack did finally have their quarrel. 'Catherine,' he said after a mostly silent evening at the safe house, 'I want you to listen to me, really listen. We have to go away from Los Angeles. Paterson can't reach you over a distance, you said, right? Then let's make it a real distance. Chicago. Or New York. We'll start a new life where he can't reach us.'

'And what if he gets strong enough to find me there?' she asked. 'What then? We run to London? South America? The moon?'

'If we have to. We'll go wherever he can't find us.'

She shook her head. 'It's no use. The answer is to see him in prison, if not dead.'

'Catherine, you're just one woman — a stubborn one and a wonderful one, but there are limits to what you can do alone, and the time may have come for you to face them,' Jack said angrily.

'I'm not alone,' she snapped, and was immediately sorry that she had been so sharp. 'Besides, wherever we go,' she said more patiently, 'he will find us eventually. He will never quit now that he knows who I am and how to project himself. Sooner or later, he'll reach me wherever I am. He's getting stronger all the time. I'll never be free of him so long as he's out there, searching for me.'

'Which makes it all the more imperative that we put you out of harm's way. All right, maybe in time he could find you, but it's only an astral projection, right? Even if he learned that you were in New York, he couldn't do anything to you without going there physically. And getting away from here does buy us time. He could be caught and in prison before he gets strong enough to track us down.'

'No, Jack. This . . . this thing that I have to do, it's a part of me now, maybe the major part.'

They regarded one another grimly for a long moment. Jack felt as if he were struggling through a quagmire, torn between his love for her and his fear of what her obsession was doing to her, to them. If she were ill, physically ill — if she had cancer, say, he would never leave her; would nurture and succor her in any way that he could. This was something else though, something he couldn't ameliorate for her, this fixation with Paterson. *That* was her cancer, and it was as malignant, as insidious as anything that might have corrupted her body. It was poisoning her — poisoning them, feeding a gulf that seemed to grow ever wider and deeper between them.

'Can't you see?' he said, sharply. 'It's not just his evil anymore. Somehow it's become yours. It's destroying you. I can't bear to watch it any longer. Every time he goes after you, every time you go after him, it's like some evil test of wills between the two of you, and I am left to stand helplessly aside and watch. It's killing me. Catherine, I beg you . . . '

'I understand how you feel.'

'Do you?' he asked, and now there was an unmistakable note of bitterness in his voice. He was convinced she had no idea how he felt. Nothing, no one, was as important to her now as Paterson. Second fiddle was not a happy instrument to play.

'Don't you see, Jack? Those children — the ones he's damaged already, and the ones he means to steal. I'm all they have.'

'Can't you see you're all *I* have?' he asked. 'Catherine, you can't bring Becky back to life.'

She tried to control the anger that flared up within her. 'Damn it, Jack, that's not fair,' she swore finally, and whirled to face him — but he had gone, the door closing softly in his wake.

She stared at it, part of her wanting to run after him, to beg him to stay. She even, for a brief moment, wondered if he could be right; if she should give up her pursuit of Paterson and just run away, run so far that he couldn't ever find her. But in her heart she knew that she could never quit so long as he was still out there, still free to do evil.

Then somehow the means to stop him must be shown to her as well, mustn't it? And hadn't the guidance she needed so often come to her in the past? She would just have to trust that it would again.

She walked into the bedroom, threw herself across the bed, and began to cry.

★　★　★

It was morning before she slept, and nearly noon by the time she woke, feeling scarcely rested, and utterly weary with living like a fugitive. And for what? she asked herself for the umpteenth time. Paterson was gone — to Mexico probably, a hundred miles and at least two hours away. She even took the chance of trying fleetingly to find him on the astral level and got only a dim image that told her clearly he was nowhere near.

To make matters worse, she had picked up a bug, had woken nauseous and barely made it to the bathroom before she lost last night's dinner. Or maybe it was the stress of her quarrel with Jack.

In any case, it was one misery too many. She made up her mind that Paterson could not be allowed to steal her life from her by default. He might win after all in the end, but she was not going to give up everything for his sake.

She called Jack at the station and was told he was in a meeting. 'Would you like his voice mail?' his secretary asked.

Catherine hesitated. Her feelings were such a muddle: frustration, anger with him for not understanding, anger and guilt with herself because at least a part of her suspected he was right. How could she say all that on his voice mail?

'No, I'll call him later,' she said instead.

*　*　*

Despite everything, Catherine found that it was astonishingly good just to be outside, in her car, moving with the traffic on the L.A. streets. It had rained early, but the rain had stopped and an erratic wind seemed determined to drive the remaining clouds away. Her spirits lifting, she promised herself that she would call Jack later in the afternoon and mend things with him. She meant to pick up the reins of her life again, instead of surrendering them to Paterson. What a fool she had been.

She drove straight to the office in Century City. She wanted work, catharsis, a chance to stretch her mental muscles. She started with the mountain of mail that had accumulated in the few days she had been off: bills, book proposals, letters. She sorted them into piles and, armed with a letter opener, started with the financial stack. She had half-opened a bank statement before she took a second look at the envelope and realized it wasn't her bank.

Fidelity Bank and Trust. It was another moment before she registered that this was the bank where Walter kept their joint account. She looked again at the address. Yes, it had been sent to the house, and both their names listed, Walter's first. Somehow this had mistakenly been forwarded with her mail.

She started to write 'forward' on the envelope and then, remembering that it was half-opened, decided instead she would drop it by the house. There were one or two things she had been meaning to pick up anyway.

She had no more than set the envelope

aside than her phone rang and to her surprise, it was Walter on the line. 'What a coincidence,' she said, meaning to mention the statement to him, but he began to talk in a hurry, his voice anxious, stressed.

'Catherine, I . . . I'm embarrassed to ask, but I need some money. Some unexpected expenses at the restaurant. I wondered if . . . ' He paused expectantly.

'Of course,' she said, surprised. Walter had always been so meticulous in handling money, she could hardly imagine him running short. Finances had never been an issue between them, however. If anything, she supposed he had been overly generous with her. 'How much do you need?'

'Five thousand,' he blurted out.

The figure was another surprise. She expected him to say a few hundred. It left her briefly speechless.

He misread the pause. 'I can pay it back out of the money from the house,' he said quickly. 'With interest. I wouldn't ask if it weren't . . . '

'No, no, that's all right. Interest won't

be necessary, and I'm not worried about your paying it back. It's only, I don't think I have that much in my account.'

'Can you spare two?'

She did a quick mental calculation. 'Yes, I think I can. I'll have to stop by the bank a little later. Did you want me to drop it off at the restaurant?'

'I'll come pick it up at your office, if that's all right. And Catherine, you are a peach. You don't know how much I appreciate this.'

'Don't give it a thought,' she assured him. It was not until he had rung off that she realized that she had forgotten to mention the bank statement.

She was still staring at the envelope, puzzling at the strangeness of Walter's behavior, when the phone rang again. This time it was a woman's voice, one she didn't recognize. 'I'm calling from Fidelity Bank and Trust,' she said.

Another coincidence? 'Yes?'

'There seems to be a slight problem with your account. It's a bit overdrawn. We wondered if you could take care of that at your earliest convenience.'

'You must mean the joint account that my husband and I keep,' Catherine said.

'Yes. That would be the one.' She rattled off an account number. Catherine jotted it down. 'It's only a few hundred, you understand. But we do like to stay on top of these things.'

'I don't understand,' she said, more to herself than to the woman on the phone.

'Well, there have been some rather large checks drawn on the account of late. Perhaps your husband wrote them, but you have seen the statement, I presume. Or if you haven't, I could send you another copy, if you like.'

The statement? 'No, that won't be necessary. I'll — '

'You really should review the charges,' the voice said.

She hung up the phone and picked up the bank statement instead and considered. In all the years she had been married to Walter, she had never even glanced at one of these statements; had always left that account entirely up to him. She'd never had any reason to distrust him in that way. Now, contemplating looking at the statement as that voice on the phone had advised her to do, she felt guilty; disloyal even, as though she were sticking her nose into Walter's business.

Hints that her mother had dropped, perhaps too casually, flashed into her mind, that Walter might have a drug problem. That, too, seemed incredible. Yet it did happen to people, she knew that much; to ordinary decent people whose descent into drug addiction started with one seemingly harmless step. Certainly he had been through a period of great stress — without, she had to add, having the great good fortune that she had had in linking up with Jack.

Her own bank didn't bother with checks at all anymore — only listed the check numbers and amounts, as she thought most banks did today — but Fidelity Bank and Trust still included both a listing of the amounts and, on a second sheet, photocopies of the checks themselves in miniature.

She looked at the debit amounts first. For the most part, they were routine. Property taxes, electric bill, water bill, gas

. . . and there, in the middle, three debits of nine thousand dollars each.

Twenty-seven thousand dollars. She looked at the second sheet, at the reproductions of the checks. There they were, three checks written to the same payee: Harvard Beerman Health Clinic.

Walter was ill, then, and had said nothing to her about it, perhaps thinking that she would have put off her decision to leave — as she would have, surely. You couldn't walk out on a sick man, a sick husband, could you, not knowing that he was ill; not even if you were in love with another man?

Only — and with this thought came once more that nagging sense of doubt, of something else amiss — Walter had health insurance, excellent and almost total coverage. They both did. There was almost nothing their insurance did not cover.

Drugs? Again that popped into her mind. Perhaps Walter did have a problem and had already faced it, had already started rehabilitation. Did their insurance cover drug treatment? She couldn't remember.

She had never heard of the Harvard Beerman Health Clinic. She looked in her desk drawers for a phone book, and was eyeing the shelves along the wall when Bill came in with some manuscripts.

'Looking for something?' he asked.

'A phone book. Would you find . . . no, wait. Here.' She wrote the name of the clinic on a piece of paper and handed it to him. 'I've got to run to my bank. See if you can find out what this place is — what kind of clinic, I mean. If they do, well, any specialized kind of treatment, or just general medicine.'

13

The bank was only a few blocks from Catherine's Century City office. She walked, hurrying against a chilling winter wind, worried thoughts blowing through her mind as she went.

She cashed a check for two thousand dollars and hurried back to her office. Bill was there before she had finished hanging up her coat.

'Harvard Beerman Health Clinic is not particularly forthcoming about their practice,' he said. 'They wanted to know what kind of problem I had, and whether I had been referred to them by anyone. That seemed to matter a lot. I don't think they take patients except by referral. But I did get you a phone number and an address.' He handed those to her.

She puzzled over the information when he had gone, and studied the address he had written down. Her Thomas's map of Los Angeles confirmed what she had already guessed, that the address was in Compton. Compton was a ghetto neighborhood, notoriously dangerous. Drugs, gangs, rampant crime. Not the sort of address she would have expected Walter to visit. Certainly not where you would expect to find an expensive clinic.

She picked up the phone, intending to call Jack, and hesitated. He would try to talk her out of what she planned to do. They would surely quarrel again.

She put the receiver back on its cradle, donned her coat again, changed from heels to walking shoes, and took the elevator to the garage.

★   ★   ★

Paterson had grown restless, not used to living cooped up with only Colley's company. A good enough partner in his way, he mostly did as he was told, and he could be surprisingly inventive when the situation called for it. Still, having him underfoot full-time could get old quickly.

His thoughts kept circling back to her: the bitch. He wanted her dead. He wouldn't rest till he had managed that, but not until he had heard her beg, beg for death. When he finally killed her, he would be doing her a favor. He wanted that so bad he could taste it.

Even those daydreams didn't satisfy him today, though. The cabin, primitive and not very big to begin with, got smaller by the hour. Christ, couldn't that TV fag afford something better? The best you could say for it was that it was a long ways from anywhere. Or anybody. No other houses along this road, nothing more than a dirt track that ended a short distance beyond O'Dell's shack; just petered out at a steep, wooded hillside that attracted not even the more adventurous hikers. Since they had been here, he hadn't heard or seen a trace of anybody except for the distant buzz of a chainsaw somewhere beyond the hill behind them.

Today there was not even that to break the silence, only a tuneless humming from Colley while he puttered around in the kitchen space — not really a separate room, just some counters along one wall with a stove and a fridge, and some cupboards overhead. Outside a woodpecker drilled at a tree, and the wind made ghostly noises in the pines. It was like being in prison.

Besides, something was gnawing at Paterson. Something to do with *her*, only he didn't know what; couldn't put his finger on it. He had been delighted that time he had popped in on her, just the way she had with him. Scared her witless, he could see that, and once again he was the one in control.

Only, he didn't know how he had done it. It was like he was thinking about her, thinking hard, and all of a sudden there he was. He had tried since, though — had given himself a headache thinking about her — and gotten nothing for his trouble. A couple of times he almost thought he could see her at a distance, like she was out there in a deep fog, but he couldn't reach her.

He gave a snort of disgust and jumped up from the sofa where he was sitting, watching a grainy image on the little black-and-white TV. One lousy channel was all that the rooftop antenna brought in, and half the time you couldn't even watch that, it was so bad.

'Get your coat,' he said to Colley. 'Let's go for a ride.'

Colley glanced at the pale light struggling through the closed curtains over the windows. 'Now?' he asked. 'It's still daylight, Trash. Suppose someone sees us?'

'Who, one of those wild donkeys? They was the last ones to mosey by. Besides, the sun's mostly down. By the time we hit L.A., it'll be dark.'

'Sure, but ain't it dangerous — ' Colley started to argue.

'Anyone tries to look too close, I'll slide down in the seat. It's my face plastered on TV. No one's looking for you, are they? Let's go. You drive.'

★   ★   ★

At one time Compton had been an upper-middle-class bedroom community for Los Angeles proper, a California stew of architecture: Victorians, Spanish bungalows, ranch, saltboxes. A tide of immigrants had built for themselves imitations of the homes they had left behind.

That had been several decades ago. In the intervening years the once proud-looking bungalows and ranches had mostly disappeared or morphed into gas stations, thrift stores, groceries. The Victorians and the saltboxes were apartment buildings and boarding houses now, with graffiti-stained storefronts at the street level. More than a few of them were boarded up and empty.

Catherine's Jaguar was decidedly conspicuous. Knots of idlers on street corners smoked and watched with undisguised curiosity as she drove by. A wino slept in a doorway, and a ragged-looking creature of indeterminate sex pushed a heavily laden shopping cart.

She nearly missed the Harvard Beerman Medical Clinic. It sat behind stone walls and a heavy wire gate that presumably closed at night, which was rapidly drawing near. The clinic itself was a one-story stucco, faded pink, with glass-brick windows. The ghosts of graffiti had bled through the thin coating of paint that had been daubed over it. Some straggly bushes lined the front on either side of an entrance door, and a conspicuously unswept parking lot ran along one side, ending at an alley. A gray Honda Civic and a big black Mercedes Sedan, altogether too showy for Compton, sat side by side at the nearer end of the parking lot; and at the far end, like a social outcast, was a dirty white Toyota.

Catherine parked in the middle. If anyone came shopping for wheels, they would hopefully find one of the other cars more attractive than her Jaguar.

She entered a waiting room that belied the expensive treatment that Walter must have gotten here: the sooty walls badly needed a fresh coat of paint. A chipped plastic table strewn with tattered and outdated magazines sat between a pair of sagging chairs, and the floor was covered with well-worn linoleum.

A buzzer sounded as she came in, and a frosted-glass panel slid open in the wall facing the door. A receptionist in a pink uniform looked her over quickly and thoroughly, and a young woman standing behind her paused in her filing to stare in undisguised curiosity. Walk-ins were apparently not common here.

'Yes?' the woman in pink asked. The monosyllable was carefully neutral. A placard on the desk identified her as Miss Griff.

'I'd like to see the doctor,' Catherine said.

'Are you a patient?' The tone said clearly that Miss Griff did not think so.

'No,' Catherine said.

Before she could explain further, the receptionist said, 'We aren't taking any new patients,' and started to slide the glass panel shut.

'Wait.' Catherine put a hand on the pane to stop it. 'I wanted to talk about my husband. He *is* a patient, I believe.'

'Name?'

'Desmond. Walter Desmond.'

She saw something register in the woman's eyes before she gave her head an emphatic shake and said, 'Sorry, we don't have a patient by that name.'

'Desmond,' the girl at the file cabinet said. 'Wasn't that . . . ?'

'We don't have a patient by that name,' the receptionist repeated firmly. She snatched up some papers from her desk and thrust them at the girl. 'Donna, give these to Doctor Beerman. And then you can take your dinner break.'

This time the glass panel shut fully and firmly.

14

Sitting in the parking lot, twilight settling around the car like a fog, Catherine tried to make sense of what had just taken place. She understood that doctors needed to be concerned about patient confidentiality, but this seemed to have gone far beyond that. She was certain the receptionist had lied. There had been that flicker of recognition before she insisted that Walter was not a patient. And surely the filing clerk, Donna, had started to say something entirely different.

Donna came out a side door in the clinic and hurried head-down to the Toyota at the far end of the lot, not seeming even to notice the Jaguar parked forty feet away. The Toyota's engine sputtered, coughed a time or two, and finally caught. Donna backed the car out of its space, turned, and drove into the alley.

Catherine followed her down the alley and out onto a busy street. Evening traffic was thick and she wondered if she would be able to keep the Toyota in sight, but fortunately the drive was a short one. Three blocks away, Donna turned into the parking lot of El Palacio, an anything but palatial-looking Mexican restaurant.

Catherine parked a few spaces away from her. She waited for Donna to go inside, and gave her time enough to order. The lot was mostly empty. She took a bundle of twenties out of her purse and shoved them into her pocket. She was careful to lock her car door and gave the badly lit lot a quick look around before she walked briskly past steam-frosted windows to the entrance and went in.

The small dining room was damp and overheated, with a smell of old grease and exuberant spices. A long window opened to a kitchen where several women sweated and worked energetically, hardly paying any attention to her entrance. A jeans-clad waitress with ketchup-colored antlers on her head looked her over and made a motion with her hands that Catherine took to mean 'sit anywhere.'

Donna was at a small table along one

wall, reading a paperback novel and sipping a beer. Catherine took a breath and approached her quickly. She had slipped into the chair opposite before Donna even noticed her.

'I'm sorry to intrude,' Catherine said, 'but I wonder if you could spare me a minute?'

Donna gaped, startled. Too-narrow eyes blinked when they saw her and then narrowed still further.

'You're that woman, like, at the clinic,' she said.

'Yes, and I . . . I do apologize for sneaking up on you like this. It's just . . . well, it's very important.'

Donna clamped her mouth shut and closed her paperback novel. 'Excuse me,' she said and started to get up, chair scraping.

'No, wait, please.' Catherine put a hand over the one with the book. 'I won't take but a moment, I promise. And I would be ever so grateful if you would just talk to me.' With her other hand, she took the twenties out of her pocket and laid them atop the table, her fingers not quite covering them. Donna's eyes flicked to the money and stayed there. She sat back down and took another sip of her beer.

The waitress approached and set a plate of chicken with rice in front of Donna, her eyes briefly registering the money under Catherine's fingers. 'Anything else?' she asked, eyes sliding from Donna's face to Catherine's and back to the money. The felt antlers drooped and bobbed.

'Just coffee for me,' Catherine said. Donna shook her head. *At least*, Catherine thought, *I've got her attention*. She waited until the waitress left before continuing.

'It's just that,' she said, dropping her voice to a conspiratorial level, 'well, I thought that the other woman back there at the clinic, the nurse . . . '

'Miss Griff? She's a bitch.' Donna's eyes remained glued to the money on the table. 'And she's not a nurse either, not a real one.'

Catherine smiled faintly and nudged the bills a little further across the table with the tips of her fingers. 'I'm sure she had her reasons for shunting me off. Her

216

orders, probably. But I'm just so worried — about my husband, I mean. I'm afraid he's seriously ill, and he won't talk to me about it. I thought if I could talk to his doctor . . . but, well . . . ' She let her voice trail off.

'It isn't like that,' Donna said. 'Your husband wasn't even, like, the patient. He just came in with his brother; it was his brother that was the patient. But it was, you know, your husband who paid for him.'

'His brother?'

'Mike Something. He was, like, his half-brother, I think. Anyway, I remember they didn't have the same last name. They didn't look alike, either. But, you know, half-brothers don't, do they?' She shrugged and pulled her eyes up at last to Catherine's face. As if of their own accord, her hand with its chewed nails rested on the table top, then moved slightly in the direction of the bundle of twenties.

Walter had no brother, half or otherwise. They had often talked of the fact that they had both been only children.

'And was he, this brother, was he very ill?' she asked.

A shake of the head. 'Not at all. It was, you know, he had some work done. Like, cosmetic work — that's what they do there, the doctors at the clinic. Mostly cheap boob jobs, collagen, nose jobs. They fixed his nose, I remember. Not, like, a nose job, I mean; not a regular nose job. Just, when he came in it was all bent to the side, you know, like it had been broken or something. And they took a mole off his chin. I don't know exactly what all. I wasn't . . . are you all right?'

'Yes, I'm fine,' Catherine managed to say.

''Cause you looked like you were about to pass out. Look, let me get you some water or something.' Donna started to get up again and, remembering, paused to snatch up the money and shove it into a pocket of her jacket.

Catherine got to her feet, almost colliding with the waitress bringing her coffee. 'No, thank you, I have to go.' She tossed a couple of ones on the table for the coffee, then walked quickly away, out of the restaurant, heart pounding.

The waitress stared after her. 'What

was that all about?' she asked.

Donna took the money from her pocket and unfolded it. Five of them. A hundred bucks. Not bad. She shrugged and said, 'Some society bitch slumming . . . who knows.'

★ ★ ★

In her car Catherine sat and stared into the darkness. Walter and Paterson? It wasn't possible, surely? The man who had kidnapped his daughter? She couldn't believe it.

Was there some other connection? She thought of Walter hiding something in that space under the floor in his office. Once again, drugs came into her mind. Maybe the answer was there.

At the first stoplight, she called Walter on his cell phone and, when he answered, asked if he had gotten the money she had left for him.

'Yes, Catherine. Thank you so much. I'll pay you back, I promise.'

'I'm glad I could help. Sorry I missed you, but something came up.' There were kitchen noises in the background, telling her he was at the restaurant. That was her real reason for phoning him, and no need now to ask. The house was empty. That was what she wanted to know.

She caught the Santa Monica Freeway west, glad to be out of Compton, took Westwood Boulevard off the freeway and drove north: toward the house that she had shared for so many years with Walter. The house where, she hoped, her questions would be answered.

★   ★   ★

Something was wrong, Jack told himself. From the moment he had stepped into his office after his meeting; from the moment the lights seemed to flicker, casting an eerie yellow glow briefly over the room, alarms bells had gone off in his mind.

His first thought was of Catherine. He had agonized the remainder of the night over their quarrel, desperately trying to find some middle ground that they could settle in, and finding himself inevitably back at the same stalemate.

He had started to call her before leaving for work, and put it off. He told himself that it was consideration for the fact that she might be sleeping in, but it was sheer cowardice. He was afraid she might not want to talk to him, might never want to talk to him again. Cowardice and frustration, because he still had no argument that would convince her to give up her pursuit of Trash Can Paterson. He put the call off, hoping that some inspiration would come to him.

Now, however, the warning bells were too loud to ignore. He called the number at the safe house, but there was no answer. He listened in mounting frustration as the phone rang again and again. On a hunch, he called her apartment. Nothing. He hung up and checked his voice mail. Nothing there either. He tried her office, and when she wasn't in, asked to talk to Bill.

'She was here,' Bill said. 'She left a couple of hours ago.'

'Did she say anything about where she was going?'

'Not really. She asked me to look up a clinic in Compton. The . . . let me think . . . the Harvard Beerman Clinic. She might have gone there.'

Jack hung up the phone, more puzzled and worried than ever. Compton? Catherine's doctor had offices in Century City, not far from where she worked. Why would she go to a clinic in Compton, of all places?

Still — a medical problem. Maybe a different doctor? You couldn't hold the location against someone. And no real evidence that she had gone there anyway. That might have been mere coincidence, or something to do with a book. More than likely, Catherine had given in to the frustration and boredom of being confined, and her unhappiness over their spat, and had simply gone out for a breather.

That strange yellow light, like lightning, flickered again.

He dialed Chang's number.

★   ★   ★

Sitting at a stoplight in Hollywood, Chang listened with a growing sense of unease to Jack's worried explanation. She had been about to call both of them with her good news: O'Dell had completely caved when they had showed up with their warrant; had tearfully told them everything; had fingered Paterson as his supplier, both for drugs and for kid-porn.

'He's evil,' he blubbered while the uniforms bagged and cataloged his collection. 'I should never have gotten mixed up with him.'

Amen to that, Chang had thought, but she could find no sympathy in her heart for O'Dell. He had been an all-too-willing participant, as far as she could see. Without the collusion of people like him, the Patersons and his ilk would be out of business before they started.

She had left Conners to book the actor and was on her way back to her office, to coordinate with the King for a warrant to enter the Big Bear cabin, when she got the call from Jack. The news that Catherine had disappeared — into Compton? — took precedence over warrants. Paterson thought

223

he was safe in Big Bear. He would stay on ice for a few more hours. Catherine AWOL was another matter.

'She's not at the safe house?' she asked.

'She doesn't answer the phone,' he said. 'I haven't actually been yet.' He paused briefly. 'We had a quarrel. A stupid one.'

'Meet me there,' she said. The quarrel wasn't any of her business; Catherine's whereabouts were. The light had turned green and the driver behind her began to honk insistently.

She gave him the bird and hung a right at the next corner, already punching numbers into her cell phone.

'Shoot-out at the O.K. Corral,' she said when Conners answered.

15

Walter had no sooner ended his call with Catherine than his cell phone rang again. It was the voice he dreaded. He prayed each time that this would be the last, and knew in his heart that it would never end.

'I'm on the freeway, heading into town,' Paterson said. In the background Walter could hear the roar of engines, horns honking, the woosh of thousands of tires on pavement. 'I need that five grand.'

'I haven't got that much, Trash.' He hated himself for the whine that crept into his voice. 'Like I told you, I'm all tapped out. When the house gets sold, then I can . . . '

'I can't wait for no blasted house to sell. I need some money now. How much have you got?'

'Two thousand. That's all I could get. I'm broke, I tell you. And something else, Trash . . . ' He hesitated, fearing the reaction he would get, but he forced himself to say it anyway. 'I've been thinking about this long and hard. I'm giving it up.'

Paterson's voice was sharp. 'What do you mean, giving it up? Giving what up?'

'All of it.' Walter's voice broke in a sob. One of the grill cooks glanced in his direction. Walter sniffled loudly and got himself under control. 'I'll give you the two thousand,' he said in a lowered voice, 'and then I'm getting rid of all my stuff. I'm going to burn it. It's sick, man. *I'm* sick. I can't live with myself anymore. I can't live with what I've done. I'm going to burn everything, and then I'm turning myself in. To the police.'

'The police? Are you crazy? What about me? Hell, here I have been, nothing but a friend to you all this time — anything you wanted, nothing was too good for you — and you're talking about turning on me, turning me over to the cops?'

'Not you,' Walter insisted. 'I won't say a word about you or Colley, I swear it. I wouldn't ever do that. I just . . . I got to do it, man. I've got to get this off my conscience. It's killing me. I'm dying from inside.'

'Look. First place, you can't burn DVDs; they won't melt.' He had no idea if that was true or not, but it sounded right, and anyway Desmond was dumb; he wouldn't know any better. 'Okay, so say you don't want the stuff around anymore. I'll take it off your hands; you just hand it all over to me and it's gone. Hell, I'll even get you some of your money back. Not all of it, but some.'

'I don't care about the money.'

'Well if you turn yourself in to the police, you're going to need money for a lawyer, that's for sure. Lots of money. Look, where are you now?'

'I'm at the restaurant, but I'm just getting ready to go home. I'm going to do it now, before I turn chicken.'

'Okay, calm down, calm down. Listen, I'll meet you there, at your place. We'll talk about all this. Don't do anything till I get there, okay?' Walter hesitated. 'Okay?' Paterson insisted.

Walter ran the back of his hand across his runny nose. 'Okay. And, Trash, I mean it — I'm not going to say anything to the cops about you, not a word.'

Paterson ended the call. 'Head for Desmond's place,' he told Colley. 'Quick like a rabbit.' His mood was ferocious. Everything had gone wrong, and he knew exactly who was to blame. But he couldn't have her husband screwing things up either.

'What are you going to do, Trash?' Colley asked, automatically picking up speed.

'What the hell do you think I'm going to do?' Paterson reached into the glove box and took out the .38, checking to make sure it was loaded. 'He's dead meat.'

16

Catherine parked the car half in, half out of the garage and called the house number yet again on her cell phone. She could actually hear the kitchen phone ringing inside.

She felt a prickling at the back of her neck as she got out of the car. Paterson, somewhere close? She heard the sound of an approaching car and held her breath, but it went on by, splashing a street-side puddle of rainwater.

She went in through the kitchen, leaving the garage door open so that if he should come home, Walter would know she was here. Better to confront him than to have him call the police to report a burglary in progress. If everything she suspected was somehow a horrible mistake, she certainly did not want the police involved in it.

She tossed her jacket on a chair, hardly glancing at the disarray, and went directly to Walter's office. Even living alone, he would probably not have abandoned his safe hiding place. That sort of habit did not die easily.

The carpet on the floor of the closet was loose. She pulled it back, to reveal a trapdoor. The space below was crude, unfinished, just dust-covered boards and wooden beams. Nestled in the gap between the beams was a small cardboard box. She lifted it out, dreading what she might find, and opened the flaps on top.

A gun lay inside. She hadn't known Walter even owned a gun. It was impossible for her to imagine him using it.

Next to the gun was a small plastic bag half-filled with white powder. Cocaine? she wondered. Speed? She was woefully ignorant about such things, but Chang would know. And anyway, that wasn't what she was looking for. Just for the moment she couldn't have cared less about any drug problem of Walter's. If there were anything that evidenced a link between him and Paterson, this was where it would be hidden.

Beneath the plastic bag were a couple of DVDs, unlabeled, and a manila envelope. The envelope was filled with pictures. She slid them out and looked at the one on top.

Her stomach gave a warning turn. She gasped aloud. Though she had never before seen anything like this, she knew exactly what she was looking at. Chang had called it 'kiddie porn,' but that label was altogether misleading. It sounded too cute, too innocent, for the filth she held in her hands.

How, she wondered dazedly, could anyone find this sexually exciting? Yet it was self-evident that *someone* must. This clearly was the business that drove Paterson and Colley: producing just such horrors as these pictures and, she was sure without even looking at them, the videos as well. This was why they needed children, needed to steal them — because how else to recruit these poor, tortured innocents? She leafed through the photographs, having to force herself to look at them when her eyes wanted to slide away. Little girls, and little boys as well. No gender discrimination in this hell, she thought grimly.

She groaned aloud and let the pictures fall from her hands. They fluttered to the floor like leaves from a dying tree.

It was horrible enough to contemplate what Paterson and Colley had done, were still doing. That Walter had kept these pictures, kept them hidden away here in this little cache, told her everything. She had lived with a stranger for years; shared his home, his bed, borne a child to him. And here, for the first time, she was seeing who he really was. A part of her hated not only him, but herself as well for being such a fool, for unwittingly providing him with a cover of innocence that had allowed him to practice his vice undetected, even unsuspected. With a loud sob, she buried her face in her hands.

'Catherine?' Walter said from outside the room. He appeared in the door and saw her kneeling by the closet, his eyes taking in the exposed cubbyhole, the cardboard box, the photos strewn on the floor. 'Oh, hell,' he said.

'Yes, Walter, hell.' She got slowly to her feet, hardly noticing that her legs had gone stiff from kneeling on the hard floor. 'That is exactly what I am looking at, at a window into hell.'

He stood motionless, hands hanging helplessly at his sides, and began to cry quietly, tears rolling down his cheeks. 'I wanted to tell you. For so long, I wanted to, but I couldn't. How could I?'

'How, indeed? How could one explain anything like this — ' She leaned down to snatch up a handful of the photographs. ' — to any sane person? What? Why? How?'

'It was drugs. Cocaine.' He paused for her to say something.

'Go on,' she said in an icy voice. 'I want you to make me understand what could have brought you to this. How could cocaine, how could any drug, result in these pictures?'

'You remember, three years ago,' he said, speaking in an earnest voice as if he truly wanted to make it clear to her, 'when I started up the restaurant, I was working such long hours, night and day it

233

seemed? One of the cooks offered me some cocaine. Have you ever . . . ?'

She shook her head and said nothing.

'Well, it's hard to describe exactly. It picks you up, like a super-tonic. Everything goes faster. And at first it helped, I couldn't believe how well. It gave me the energy I needed, and it seemed like I could go on forever.

'It was just a little each time to start; a couple of lines once, maybe twice an evening. After a while, though, I needed more to do the job, and more still. And finally the cook said it would be cheaper and simpler if I got it myself, and he hitched me up with a supplier. I started getting it by the ounce — it was cheaper, like he'd said, and I had all I needed all the time. The dealer was there for me whenever I needed him.'

'Paterson,' she said, her voice even, emotionless.

He blinked, surprised that she knew the name. 'Yes, Paterson. Trash Can, they call him. How do you . . . ?' But her look stopped his question. He hesitated but when she said nothing, he went on.

'Well, that worked for a while. I'd buy it from him, and sometimes we'd do it together at his place, and listen to music and talk. He seemed like such a great guy. He made me feel . . . I don't know. Smart, important, special. Our marriage wasn't, you know . . . Things had long since died out for us. No, no, it wasn't our marriage, it wasn't you. I know that. Paterson is to blame, he's the one who . . . '

His voice broke. He swallowed hard. 'Well, one night he told me someone owed him for a bunch of drugs and didn't have the money, so they paid him off with a collection of pornography, and that some of it was pretty weird. He played on my curiosity until I insisted I see it for myself. I was high. You think funny when you're on the stuff.

'Anyway, there was a lot of the usual sort of thing. It was okay, some of it was pretty good, but I couldn't see what he meant about weird. Then he showed me this one movie . . . it's there, in the hole. It . . . it disgusted me, Catherine, honestly it did. But, God forgive me, it excited me

235

too. I couldn't help it. I got turned on watching it. I know it's sick, but we can't help how we are, can we?'

She came a step toward him and brandished the stack of photographs. 'Tell me Becky isn't in these pictures.'

He began to sob then, softly at first and then louder, his tears streaming unchecked, his nose running. 'I couldn't help it,' he said between choking sobs. 'They black-mailed me. There were pictures of me with this little girl. I was in some of them. I swear to God I didn't even remember them being taken. I don't know when or how it happened, but it was me, you could recognize me right off. I must have been totally wasted. Anyway, they showed me these pictures; they threatened me with them, if I didn't . . . they made me . . . that day . . . '

She suddenly realized where this was leading. Her heart seemed to stop. In her worst nightmare she could not have imagined this. 'You set her up, didn't you?' she demanded, her voice little more than a hoarse whisper, the words coming only with great difficulty. 'You let them take her that day.'

His sobs became a bleat of pain. 'They promised me they wouldn't hurt her. They swore it. They were just going to take pictures, was all. They even let me be there, so I could be sure, so I could see for myself they didn't hurt her. I would never have agreed otherwise, I swear it. I said I would have to be there. I insisted.'

The light. It was there in the room, growing rapidly brighter, beginning to swirl around her. She found it increasingly difficult to keep him in focus. She knew what it meant, knew she was being called somewhere; but she couldn't go, not now. She had to know the rest, all of it, no matter what it cost her. She pushed the light away from her with her mind.

'Wouldn't hurt her? Are you mad? How could you think this — ' She waved the photos at him. ' — wouldn't hurt her? And they killed her, didn't they? Were you there when they did that, too? Did you not think that hurt her? Me? You?'

'No!' he shouted at her. 'I swear I wasn't there when . . . I left. I couldn't stand to watch, it was . . . I wanted it to stop, but they wouldn't. They laughed at me; told me if I wasn't man enough to get out. And I did.'

'And you left her there?'

'Only, she had seen me, Catherine. She knew I was there. She called me 'Daddy.''

It broke in her then. A moan came out of her like the sound of death. She flung the pictures in his face and ran at him, slapping him with all her strength, pounding his chest with her fists, her own tears pouring down now.

'God damn you, God damn you straight to hell, Walter!'

'Yes, yes,' he sobbed, and sank to his knees before the fury of her attack. 'Hit me, kick me, *kill me* — in the name of heaven, I want to die.'

She stepped back from him, panting for breath, like she had just finished a ten-kilometer run. 'You shall, Walter, you shall, I promise you that.'

He sat on his knees, head bent, sobbing helplessly. She turned from him — couldn't bear the sight of him, the sound of his sobs. She left the room, went to where she had tossed her jacket and fished her cell phone out of the pocket.

'Where are you?' Chang answered the call at once.

'I'm at Walter's, at the house. I need to see you. I — '

This time the light would not be denied. It consumed her, blinding her, and inside her head a voice shouted, *He's here!*

The warning was too late. A voice behind her, a real voice, said, 'Put down the phone.'

17

'Paterson.' She spoke the name aloud. He was there, and Colley just behind him. She hadn't heard them come in. A wave of terror swept over her and settled like ice in her veins.

'Catherine?' Chang's anxious voice sounded faintly from the cell phone. 'Paterson? He's there?'

'Yes,' Catherine said.

Paterson gestured with the gun in his hand. 'Hang it up. Put it down.'

Catherine hesitated, not so much wanting to defy him as simply too frozen to move.

'You bitch.' He strode to her and snatched the phone from her hand, flinging it to the floor, and struck her hard across the face with the back of his hand. She reeled and crashed into the wall. 'I'm going to make you pay for everything you've done to me.'

'Leave her alone,' Walter said from the

doorway of his office. He had the gun from the cubbyhole in his hand. 'Do whatever you want with me, but leave her alone.'

Colley took a step in Walter's direction and Walter fired. With a yelp of pain, Colley staggered and fell onto the sofa, knocking over the lamp beside it. But before Walter could turn back to Paterson, Paterson had shot him. Walter gave a moan and dropped his gun, clutching at the red stain that quickly spread across his chest.

'Catherine,' he gasped. He tottered a step in her direction before his legs gave out and he fell face-down, his hands splayed toward her.

Catherine screamed. 'You've killed him!' she shouted, and threw herself at Paterson, hitting his face and chest with all her strength. Her attack surprised him. The gun fell from his hand and Catherine dropped to her knees and snatched it up, but Paterson was too quick for her. He kicked it out of her hand and yanked her violently to her feet, pinning her against his chest despite her struggles.

'A wildcat, ain't you? Over him? He ain't worth it. Anyway, he had it coming.' Paterson sneered down at Walter. 'Stupid bastard. Quit struggling or I'll bust you again. Get up, Colley, you're not dead. And hand me that gun.'

'He got my leg, Trash Can,' Colley whined, but he got up as he was ordered, trying to stanch the flow of blood from a wound on his thigh, and retrieved Paterson's gun.

Catherine had stopped struggling but she was still breathing heavily. Oddly, she felt less frightened now. 'Go ahead, kill me,' she said.

'Oh, no, bitch, that'd be too easy. I've got better plans for you. I've always wanted to film a snuff movie, and I just found me my leading lady. By the time I'm through with you, you'll be begging to die.'

Her cell phone rang. He put a booted foot on it and ground it to pieces. 'Colley, get them pictures, the movies, all of it. And be quick.'

Holding a hand to his wounded leg, Colley limped into the other room, blood dripping through his fingers onto the carpet. Paterson snatched up Catherine's jacket from the chair and flung it at her. 'Put that on, I don't want you catching a cold. You're an ass-et now,' he added, making an obscenity out of the word.

Outside, stumbling down the steps, Catherine wondered if she could get away from him and make a run for it, but he held her arm in a fierce grip. She looked desperately toward the street, but the stone wall and the citrus trees that had always provided such welcome privacy in the past screened her as well from any likelihood of neighbors seeing them.

It had begun to rain again while she was inside, a steady drizzle that already was collecting in puddles. Walter's Buick sat beside the Jaguar in the garage, and behind that sat a battered gray van.

He threw open the rear door of the van and shoved her violently inside and slammed the door shut. 'Get in back with her,' he ordered Colley.

'My leg's hurting, Trash,' Colley whined, climbing in alongside Catherine and using his hands to pull his wounded leg inside. Paterson swung himself into the driver's seat and fired up the engine. They reversed into the street, and Catherine braced herself to jump from the van. But Paterson, looking over his shoulder to back up, shook his head warningly.

'Don't even think about it,' he said. 'I'd run you down before you got ten feet.'

She closed her eyes and tried to shut out the pain in her jaw where Paterson had struck her. Despair engulfed her. She thought of Walter, poor foolish Walter. He had been no match for Paterson's evil. It had consumed him. He was dead now, and she could even pity him, though she could not forgive. To the end, he had blamed everyone and everything else for his failing. He had died believing that none of it was his fault. God would judge him now.

She had no hope that her fate would be any better. She knew at least what a snuff movie was: a film of someone being murdered, the death recorded for whatever sort of ghoul found that exciting. No doubt it would be a slow, horrible death.

No, she thought suddenly, fiercely. No, that mustn't happen. She *had* died before, and she had been sent back, been given a special gift, all for a purpose: to stop them.

But how?

★ ★ ★

The first thing they saw was Walter's body on the floor, the gun nearby, the blood staining the carpet.

'Oh, God,' Jack cried, and then, 'Catherine! Catherine!' He ran through the house, from room to room, calling her name and looking for her. 'She's not here. They've taken her.'

Conners had paused to take in the filth and disorder in the kitchen. 'Wow, I wonder if Martha Stewart has an emergency number?' he said. He followed the trail of blood droplets into what appeared to be a home office, half-expecting to find another body, but there was no one there. He spotted a photograph half under the desk and stooped to pick it up, grimacing in disgust.

'Check it out,' he said, handing the photo to Chang as she entered the room.

'The husband? Into kiddies?'

'It explains a lot,' he said. 'Like the difference in their m.o. when his daughter was snatched.'

'He set it up,' she said in a burst of understanding. 'Damn. I'm sorry the bastard is dead.'

'Where . . . ?' Jack said from the doorway, but she gave him a wait-a-sec gesture.

'Get the black-and-whites on their way,' she told Conners, 'but tell them it's F.B.I. business. Touch nothing. I'll get one of our agents here pronto, but I need you to secure the scene till he gets here.'

'Where will you be?' Conners asked.

'We're headed for Big Bear,' she told him, already on the run, signaling for Jack to follow her.

*   *   *

The van rocked as Paterson swung onto a freeway at high speed, skidding slightly on the rain-slick ramp, and gunned his way into the stream of traffic. The Santa Monica Freeway, heading east. To Big Bear? Catherine wondered. She had thought Paterson was in Mexico — had seen dirt roads and shacks — but, she realized belatedly, that could describe Big Bear, too.

By now, Chang had surely reached the house. How could Catherine alert her? She closed her eyes and suddenly she was in the back seat of the Bronco, Chang at the wheel and Jack in the passenger's seat. She leaned forward and tried to tap Jack on the shoulder, but of course her hand went through him. Nor could she make any sound. How in the name of heaven was she to communicate?

She looked long and hard at the back of his neck. This had worked in the quietness of his office and her apartment, but then it had been little more than a game. Could she make him aware of her presence here, now?

'What if they've already skipped out of Big Bear?' Jack asked.

Chang swerved out of the way of another approaching black-and-white. 'They don't know we've busted O'Dell, so they still think his place is safe. I'll give you odds that's where they're taking Catherine,' Chang said with more confidence than she felt. She had gambled on Paterson's ignorance once before, with disastrous results.

He turned toward her and his glance fell on the back seat — and he saw, to his astonishment, Catherine sitting there. She nodded her head frantically.

'Big Bear?' he asked, and she nodded her head up and down again. In the next instant, she was gone.

'Yes, Big Bear,' Chang said, puzzled. 'Isn't that what we've been talking about?'

'Yes. Yes, Big Bear,' he said in an excited voice. 'Fast as you can!'

18

Colley was shaking her. 'Damn it, I told you not to let her go to sleep, Colley,' Paterson said from the front seat, slapping the steering wheel with one hand. 'For Christ's sake, do whatever you got to do to keep her awake.'

Catherine sank back against the seat, letting her entire body grow limp.

'Keep your eyes open,' Colley ordered.

She obeyed, looking straight ahead, watching the freeway signs rushing toward them in the rain-streaked wind-shield and sailing past. Yes, she had been right: they were on the I-10 now, heading east toward San Bernardino, and beyond that the mountains and Big Bear.

Paterson maneuvered the van into the fast lane. It would be forty-five minutes or more before they left the freeway, maybe an hour in this driving rain, in the dark. For the first time since Paterson had flung her into the van, however, she felt hope stirring within her. She thought wryly that Paterson had made a mistake in bringing her along alive.

Paterson rammed the heel of his hand down on the horn to warn an errant pickup truck out of his way and veered around it, tires momentarily losing their grip on the wet pavement. He swore under his breath and brought the van under control.

The rain came down harder, wipers struggling to keep the windshield clear. He turned them up to the fastest setting, and cursed again. Ahead of them, brake lights flashed as the traffic began to slow in the downpour.

Fifty-five minutes later, they veered off the freeway at Redlands and in a few minutes more they were on Route 38, the two-lane road that twisted and climbed its way into the mountains. As they drove higher, the rain on the windshield turned to sleet and soon after that to snow.

The road would take them directly into Big Bear, but Catherine was sure that the town itself was not their destination. These men would not want neighbors close by. They needed a place off to itself.

Which meant that somewhere between here and Big Bear they would leave this highway. The Big Bear area was streaked with roads and lanes, some of them little more than trails that led into the forests to isolated cabins where one could live unnoticed for weeks, months even.

Did Chang already know where they were headed? She must have, mustn't she, to have started out on her own for Big Bear? Catherine glanced surreptitiously at her watch. How far behind her could they be? Twenty minutes, maybe? Surely no more than half an hour.

The higher they climbed, the harder the snow fell, a dancing curtain of white in the twin tunnels created by their headlights. Paterson was forced to slow down, cursing non-stop as he did so. The road had been recently cleared, but already the new snow had begun to stick. The rear end of the van skidded sideways.

Catherine closed her eyes and tried to send herself swiftly to Jack and Chang. She had a brief glimpse through the windshield of Chang's Bronco and saw the freeway sign for Redlands. They were gaining ground. She opened her eyes back in the van, and suppressed a smile.

Paterson yanked his head around, his eyes narrowed. 'What are you doing?' he demanded. He closed his own eyes for a second. 'Somebody's following us, ain't they? You've tipped 'em off, haven't you? I ought to . . . ' He lifted the gun as if to strike her with it, and she cringed, but the blow did not come. 'Let 'em try to find us,' he said with a smug expression. 'You can't talk to them, can you? You can't steer the car for them. For all I care, you can go sit on his lap; that won't tell them diddly.'

He stopped once for Colley to put the chains on the tires. Even so, they were crawling now on their increasingly steep way up the mountain. Paterson drove in the middle of the road. Catherine glanced out the window at the sheer drop just beyond the edge of the road, and hoped they didn't meet any oncoming traffic on one of the curves.

'What's that up ahead?' Colley suddenly asked, alarmed. There were people and cars in the road, tail-lights and hazard lights blinking. Red and blue Highway Patrol lights flashed a warning. A uniformed officer stepped into the center of the road and held up a hand as they neared.

'It's a road block, Trash.'

'Highway Patrol,' Paterson said, peering through the fogged-over windshield. 'Get her down on the floor and put that blanket over her.'

The van slowed. Highway Patrol vehicles blocked the road ahead. Half a dozen cars were pulled into a turnoff and men were putting chains on them.

'You heard the man,' Colley said, and shoved her down between the seats. He threw the blanket over her. It smelled and she had to resist the urge to sneeze.

'Clock her if you have to,' Paterson's muffled voice said.

They were barely moving now. A patrolman strolled in the van's direction. Paterson rolled down his window. 'Evening, sir,' he greeted the uniformed man with a smile, his hands gripping the wheel tensely. The officer glanced down at the tires with their chains and nodded his approval. Half the fools driving this road had to be told they needed chains.

'Where you headed?' he asked.

'Big Bear. Road's still open, isn't it?'

'It's open, but it's snowing over pretty quick. Drive carefully, now.' He waved the van on through the checkpoint. The window went up. The van crept forward, picking up speed.

Did I know him? the patrolman wondered, looking after the van. Something teased at his memory, but another vehicle was already rolling to a stop. He forgot the van and walked up to another rolled-down window. It was a cold job. He rubbed his gloved hands together. Cold and busy. He wished his shift was over.

* * *

Catherine thought briefly about screaming, but under the cover of the blanket, Colley pressed the gun against her head. She remained silent. She had no doubt that they would kill her and the highway patrolman too. The van picked up speed again, and the cold air was cut off as Paterson rolled the window back up.

'You can get up now,' Colley said, poking her with the gun and yanking the blanket off her.

She crawled back onto the seat and sneezed. In the brief moment under the blanket, she got another glimpse of Jack and Chang. They were through Redlands already, gaining on them, the four-wheel-drive Bronco able to make better time in the weather than Paterson's van could.

In the mirror, Paterson shot her an evil look. Did he know? He seemed almost to read her mind. She looked away, blowing a piece of lint off her lip, and tried to look hopeless.

★ ★ ★

It seemed an eternity later when the van swayed and tilted as it turned off the main road. Catherine peered intently through the windows, looking for sign-posts. There — a highway marker: mile thirty-one. On the opposite side of the road, a log fence with one timber fallen

255

from its place, half-buried in the snow.

Their pace slowed even more. This road was obviously unpaved under its deep blanket of snow. They were barely crawling now, the van pitching and slewing over ruts and bumps, the body groaning. Paterson wrestled with the steering wheel and flipped the headlights to bright, but they barely penetrated the curtain of white.

'Think we'll make it?' Colley asked, bracing himself against the back of the front seat as they jarred their way over some particularly large obstacle.

'Shut up, you fool,' Paterson snapped. 'I got my hands full here. You just keep your eyes on her.'

Colley glanced dutifully in her direction, but clearly he was more concerned with their progress, and almost instantly he leaned forward again to peer anxiously through the windshield. Catherine stared too, though there was little to see beyond the endless whiteness swirling in their headlights.

They hit something — a rock, Catherine thought — and bounced even harder. The van came down with a crash and stopped, wheels spinning helplessly in an effort to get traction.

'Now see what you did!' Paterson shouted. He banged his hands on the steering wheel and gunned the motor ferociously, to no avail. The van remained stubbornly where it was, hung up on a rock.

'We'll have to walk,' he said. He switched off the engine and flung his door violently open. Catherine shuddered in the onslaught of icy air.

'It's gotta be two miles from here,' Colley said. 'We'll freeze to death before we get there.'

'Well, we sure as hell will freeze to death sitting here, won't we? We got to get to that cabin.'

'Damn it to hell,' Colley said, but he climbed out and, coming around to Catherine's side of the van, yanked her door open and tugged her out. She sank shin-deep in the snow.

19

They started off, Paterson in the lead, bending into the wind that seemed to cut right through them. Colley gripped Catherine's arm tightly and followed him, limping and trying to step in Paterson's tracks. Catherine was grateful at least that Paterson had let her bring her jacket, but it was woefully inadequate for this kind of cold, and her shoes were soaked within a few steps.

Paterson plunged ahead but it was quickly clear that neither the wounded Colley nor Catherine could match his pace. He was forced to stop often, glowering impatiently at them and waiting for them to catch up.

Once Catherine tripped and, with her hands cuffed together, was unable to get a grip to steady herself. She fell to her knees in the snow.

Colley jerked her roughly to her feet. 'You think I'm carrying you, think again,' he snarled.

'You've got to take these off.' She held up the cuffs.

'Go ahead,' Paterson said impatiently, tossing him the keys. 'She ain't got nowhere to go. You hear me, Miss High and Mighty? Best thing for you is to stay with us. You try getting away, you'll end up freezing your tight ass off out there.'

She didn't bother to answer. A fresh wave of despair swept over her. He was right: she was at their mercy.

Colley took the cuffs off and she rubbed her wrists where they had chafed. *No*, she told herself ferociously, *I won't think that way*. The important thing for the moment was that she was still alive. So long as she was alive, she had a chance.

'Let's go! Move it!' Paterson snapped. He started off again in the lead. Colley gave Catherine's arm a yank, but she needed no urging. They had a destination and that meant shelter, at least, and surviving just that much longer.

She must concentrate on that, on staying alive. That was everything at the moment, just surviving. Paterson might suspect that someone was after them, but he couldn't be sure. And Jack and Chang were gaining on them — that was another thing she knew that Paterson did not. It was an advantage, if only a slim one.

She brought one foot down in front of the other, and then again, and again, and tried not to think of her toes freezing into pieces of ice.

She soon felt as if she could go no further. Beside her, Colley was reeling and stumbling; and even Paterson, who seemed to possess a supernatural energy, was beginning to flag. In the dark, in the snow, she could just make out his back ahead of them, bent over against the wind.

He suddenly stopped in his tracks, looking around like a wild animal sniffing for a scent. Were they lost, despite his macho-man confidence? she wondered.

After a moment, he pointed his chin to their left. 'It's over here,' he said, though she could see nothing but the relentless sheets of snow.

Suddenly, as if by magic, a cabin loomed through the whiteness. Colley gave a little yip of excitement and even Catherine felt her spirits rise. Whatever might happen there, at least it would be a respite from the snow and the cold.

Paterson struggled at the door with numbed fingers. Catherine dropped helplessly to her knees on a hard wooden floor, too weak for the moment even to get to her feet.

Colley shoved the door shut behind them, a dusting of snow having already followed them in. Even without any heat, the cabin was blessedly warm after what they had just endured.

'Get her on the couch,' Paterson said, and strode across to a soot-blackened fireplace where logs were already stacked waiting to be lit. He crumpled up a wad of newspaper, found a match on the mantel and lit it, and shoved it under the wood. In a minute tinder began to crackle and flame.

Having tossed her onto the couch, Colley rushed to the kitchen, snatched a can of something from one of the shelves and, hastily opening it, began to spoon the contents furiously into his mouth. The fire started, Paterson followed his example.

He opened a can and paused to give Catherine a measuring look. He thought about killing her, but somehow that idea didn't excite him the way it had before. He wasn't really a killer, except when he had to be.

The thought came to him all of a sudden that the two of them had been brought together for some other reason, sucked to one another like nails to a magnet. No, couldn't be. He shoved that thought aside. What the hell could they have to do with one another except murdering? She'd have murdered him, that was for damned sure, if he'd given her the chance.

★　★　★

The news at the chain stop-point was dispiriting. The patrolman in charge thought he recognized the pictures of Paterson and Colley. 'Two men in a van,' he said. 'About half an hour ago, maybe forty minutes.' He was sure, however, that they had been alone. 'No woman,' he repeated when Chang asked him a second time.

Had they already killed Catherine, disposed of her body somewhere between here and Los Angeles? Or simply concealed her in the van?

'Nothing we can do at this point but go on,' she said. 'And pray a lot.' Her phone rang. It was Conners. 'Where are you?' she asked.

'Right behind you,' he said. 'Your man Renner's on the scene; didn't need me. I should be gaining on you.'

'That truck four-wheel?'

'Yes. And mine's bigger than yours. Anyway, it's snowing where you're going. You'll need someone to keep you warm.'

'You're a crazy son of a bitch,' she said, but she grinned in spite of herself. She would be glad for the reinforcements.

★　★　★

To Catherine's surprise, Paterson crossed the room in three easy strides and shoved a can and a spoon into her hands. 'Here,' he said in an angry voice. He went to the shelf and got himself another can and began to eat noisily, his back to her.

She ate gratefully, hardly noticing what it was she shoveled into her mouth: some kind of soup. The most delicious soup she had ever tasted. She finished it, wiping her mouth with the back of her hand, and set the empty can on the table next to the couch. She leaned back against the couch, closing her eyes.

'Oh, no you don't.' Paterson was there in an instant. He grabbed her shoulders and shook her hard. 'You stay awake, damn you. Colley, you see to it.'

Colley sighed wearily. 'Man, I'm dead on my feet. Let me sleep a bit — just half an hour, okay? And then I'll look after her.'

'She gets to sending her mind out, you'll be more than dead on your feet. Watch her, I tell you. I got to get some sleep so I can think clear. I got to think for the both of us, don't I? That's more important than you resting your sorry butt.'

'Well I at least got to pee,' Colley said in a petulant voice. He limped into the bathroom and closed the door with a bang. They heard him urinating loudly.

Paterson stood just in front of her. She glanced up and found him studying her again with an expression she couldn't read.

'You know,' he said, 'about your little girl. It wasn't supposed to . . . well, we never did that before, offed any of them kids. It was kind of, like, an accident. It was your old man, if you want to know the truth of it. The whole business was him from the get-go. He wouldn't stop yapping about it: why didn't we, couldn't we, wouldn't it be great?' He paused, waiting for her to say something. She could only stare at him; could scarcely grasp what he was trying to say.

She swallowed. Her mouth was Saharan. When she finally did speak, the words surprised her; seemed to come unbidden, from someone other than herself: 'I want to forgive you, Mister Paterson.'

They surprised him too. He blinked, speechless for a moment, staring at her like he hadn't heard her right.

Where had they come from, those words? She had not even imagined herself saying such a thing. They had simply spilled out of her.

Yet she meant them. Or at the least, she *meant* to mean them. She might be close to death. It was even possible, and it had occurred to her before, that she had been dead all along, and everything that had happened since she had been shot was only a dream.

In either case, she was suddenly sure of one thing: she didn't want to go back into that light carrying all the hate and bitterness and anger with her. She wanted to forgive him, if only for her own sake. And perhaps, she hoped, for his as well. If she hadn't quite done that yet, if the words she had spoken were not quite yet the truth, surely that lie would do less damage to her soul than continuing to bear the bitter burden she had borne so long.

'Someone called you 'my dark angel,'' she said.

He actually grinned. 'Yeah? What does that make you? My what, my bright angel?'

The question caught her off guard. She hadn't thought of that. What was she to him? Not his angel, surely — but something, something she herself did not understand.

His grin faded. For a crazy moment he actually thought he saw, like, a halo of light around her head. What if she was some kind of angel? What if that was what had been drawing him to her, not to kill her but to . . . well, to what? An *angel*?

To her surprise, he dropped to his knees in front of her, the wooden floor creaking. 'Listen,' he said, eyes fastened on hers, 'I wish we hadn't gotten off on the wrong foot the way we did, you and me. I'm not such a bad guy once you get to know me. And . . . well, I could've made you happy. Still could.' He grinned. 'That's what I do best. Make women happy. I'm real good at it.' He reached a hand for her leg. Smiled into her eyes. In the bathroom, the toilet flushed noisily.

Without even thinking, she spat in his face. His eyes flamed, nostrils flared. The malevolence of his smile told more clearly than any words could the depth of his anger. He wiped the spittle from his face and stood. Colley came out of the bathroom and gave them a curious look.

Ignoring him, Paterson went to the fire, now casting a welcome warmth into the room, and poked violently at it. Satisfied that it was okay, he threw the poker into the bin and gave Catherine a warning glance. 'Don't try anything,' he said, and to Colley, 'Wake me up in thirty minutes. Then you can have your turn.'

He curled up on the bed, his back to them, and within minutes was snoring. Colley pulled a tattered armchair around so it was near the fire, facing Catherine. He settled himself into it, cast a resentful glance at Paterson and glowered at her. 'Ought to have killed her back then,' he mumbled, but not loud enough to disturb Paterson's sleep.

He tried to keep his eyes fixed on Catherine, but the warmth of the fire and the draining fatigue began to take their toll. His eyelids flickered. He started and gave his head a shake, and glared at her afresh.

Something stirred in the corner — some forest creature, no doubt, a mouse or a squirrel, annoyed at having its comfortable winter lodgings intruded upon. Outside, the wind howled, and the snow blew against the window in ceaseless gusts, rattling the panes.

Colley's eyes closed and stayed closed. His breathing grew deeper, more regular, and he too began to snore.

Now, Catherine thought. She closed her eyes and sent herself into the ether.

★   ★   ★

'Yipes!' Chang cried as Catherine suddenly appeared in the seat between her and Jack. The Bronco slid briefly before she got it once more under control. She took one hand off the wheel and felt in Catherine's direction. 'Oh, Lord.' Her hand went right through the apparition. 'She's like a ghost. I forget.'

'She's not physical at all,' Jack said. 'She's here to guide us.'

'How, if she can't talk and she can't take hold of anything?'

'She can nod.' He looked down at their directions. 'Highway marker mile thirty-one?'

Catherine nodded vigorously . . . and disappeared.

★   ★   ★

Paterson was shaking her violently. 'Damn you to hell, what are you doing? You're leading them here, aren't you?'

'Sleeping,' she mumbled, trying to act as incoherent as possible. It wasn't all that difficult. The fatigue almost had put her to sleep.

'Bitch.' He slapped her hard, bringing the sting of tears to her eyes. With a muttered oath, he threw her back against the sofa and dashed to the window, yanking the curtain aside to peer out as if someone might already be pulling up outside. Over his shoulder, Catherine could see only a white blur of snow in the faint light from the window and, beyond that, darkness.

He dropped the curtain and paced back and forth for several minutes, considering. Catherine reached out tentatively, trying to read into his thoughts, but that only served to draw his attention back to her. He stopped in his pacing and snapped his head around to glower at her, and seemed finally to reach a decision. He opened a closet and took out a shotgun, then propped it against the wall.

Then he grabbed her coat off the chair and flung it at her.

'Put it on.'

On the chair nearby, Colley groaned and opened his eyes. 'Man, I could sleep for a week,' he said drowsily.

'You weren't supposed to be sleeping at all. You dumb jerk, I warned you what would happen.'

'I couldn't help it, Trash. That bullet wound is hurting bad. I just closed my eyes for a minute, anyway, I swear to God.' He looked at Catherine struggling into her coat. 'What's happening?'

'I'm taking her out of here.' Paterson shrugged into his parka. 'Hurry it up,' he told Catherine.

Colley sat up, wincing. 'Where are we going?'

'Not we. You can't move fast enough like that. You wait here in case they show up. If they do, use that.' He nodded his head toward the shotgun leaning against the wall.

Colley got unsteadily to his feet. 'Hey, Trash, no way. You can't leave me behind. We're in this together.'

Paterson shot him in his other leg. Colley went down with a yelp and a crash, taking a chair with him. The fresh wound spewed blood. He swore and clutched at it. 'Jesus, Trash,' he groaned, 'what'd you go and do that for? I'm gonna bleed to death here, you bastard!'

Paterson shrugged his unconcern. 'Bleeding, frying, you're just as dead one way or the other. Come on.' He yanked Catherine to her feet and pulled her out into the snow.

20

They had stepped into a world of white, of wind-swirled snow. Paterson hesitated, looking in every direction, and began to walk as swiftly as the storm allowed up the hillside to their left.

The wind fought against them, trying to push them back, as though it resented their intrusion. Catherine struggled to keep up, her knees threatening to buckle under her. When she stumbled he jerked her roughly back to her feet. In the dark, in the snow, it was impossible to see where they were going. He seemed to be obeying some inner radar.

'We'll never make it through this,' she told him breathlessly. His only answer was to tug again at her arm and propel her forward. Her feet and hands were numb, her nose a block of ice.

The hillside grew steeper and thicker with trees, but at least they provided some break in the wind, so that it was easier for Paterson and Catherine see where to put their feet down. They skirted rocks and thin outcroppings of brush, climbing steadily and laboriously now.

Catherine stopped dead in her tracks and fell back against the rough bark of a Ponderosa pine. 'I've got to catch my breath,' she said.

Paterson gave her an angry look and was about to say something, then checked himself. He let her lean there for a minute while his eyes searched the forest around them. Dawn was near, but the pale light barely penetrated the storm.

She closed her eyes and tried again to send herself into space. 'No, you don't,' Paterson said. He took her arm again and resumed their climb. Frustrated, Catherine stumbled alongside him.

Her feet were numb, but she was afraid that if she fell or tried to stop again, he would shoot her and be done with it. Her job now was to stay alive and to delay them as much as possible in whatever way she could. Jack and Chang would find them, she was certain of that.

They came to the crest of a hill and

there, below them, a blue pick-up truck sat in a cottage driveway. They ran clumsily down to it.

★   ★   ★

The keys were not in the ignition. Of necessity, Paterson left Catherine by the truck and crept into the darkened cottage. Its door had been unlocked.

He heard snoring from the adjacent bedroom, but the keys were right there on the kitchen table. Beside them was a butcher's knife, and he took that too. What he knew, that she didn't, was that his gun was empty. The bullet he'd fired at Colley had been its last one. There were more, of course, but they were back in the van. The knife would come in handy, he was sure.

He found Catherine leaning against the truck, her eyes closed. 'Damn you!' he shouted, slapping her awake. He drew back his hand to strike her again. She cringed away from him, but instead of hitting her, he snorted in exasperation and threw open the door of the truck.

'Get in,' he ordered, brandishing the butcher's knife under her nose, 'and no funny business.'

There was a sudden crashing and thumping to their left. Paterson's head snapped around as a dark gray muzzle appeared out of the trees. Wild burros! As he watched, the rest of them trailed out of the bushes behind their leader. One or two of them cast wide-eyed glances sideways.

'Dumb critters,' Paterson said, laughing at his own skittishness. 'Shoo, git.'

He let go of Catherine's wrist just for a second. In that same instant, there was a flash of light like lightning, only brighter still. It glared off the curtain of snow, blinding both of them.

'What the hell . . . ?' He blinked, and thought for a moment he saw another woman standing there in that fierce radiance. Startled, he took a step back. *Where did she come from?*

The sudden bolt of light startled the pack of burros into flight. They stampeded in his direction, passing him so closely that one or two of them jostled against him, throwing him off balance. He fell heavily against the truck.

Run. The voice echoed inside Catherine's head. Catherine hesitated no more than a split second before she whirled away from Paterson and dashed down the driveway in the wake of the burros, in the direction of the road.

★ ★ ★

'We'll never find her in this mess,' Chang said. In the dark, in the snow, she could barely make out the pine trees that lined the road.

Jack looked frantically out his window. She had to be this way. That had certainly been her in the road a mile or two back, signaling them not to take the planned turnoff.

Chang glanced in the rear-view mirror and thought she saw a pair of headlights in the distance. Conners was gaining on them; was only a couple of miles behind the last time she'd talked to him. She'd be glad for the reinforcements, but what good would that do if they couldn't find Catherine?

'There!' Jack shouted suddenly, pointing.

Chang saw her then too, trailing a pack of stampeding burros down a driveway they had just passed — and Paterson running after her, and gaining.

She hit the brakes hard and felt the Bronco slide.

★   ★   ★

'Get back here, you bitch!' he shouted behind her, but she only drove herself harder. She heard his footsteps pounding after her. Twenty yards away, she saw a flash of red on the roadway. The Bronco. Jack and Chang. She was saved.

It passed the driveway. She gave a hoarse shout, and was rewarded with the flare of brake lights. The Bronco slid in the snow and began to back up rapidly.

Her elation turned to agony. Her feet were too numb. She was too weary. She stumbled, almost falling, and Paterson grabbed her arm, jerking her around so violently she thought her arm had been pulled from its socket. She fell against

278

him, out of breath, too weak to struggle any further. Behind her, a car door slammed and Jack shouted, 'Catherine!'

Chang was out of the Bronco while it was still rolling, and dropped into a crouch. Behind her, she heard a pickup truck sliding to a stop. Conners. Man, that boy was something! She held the Glock in both hands, but couldn't shoot because Paterson was holding Catherine in front of him.

'Don't!' she said when Jack would have dashed past her. 'He's got a knife. He'll kill her.'

Paterson grabbed Catherine's throat and forced her head back; forced her to look directly into his face, twisted with fury. 'I told you,' he hissed. 'I told you, they wouldn't never take neither of us alive.'

They were face to face, his eyes boring into hers, eyes filled with hatred . . . and with something larger than that, something she could not define.

Her 'dark angel,' Gabronski had called him. Yes, she could see it now: they had been tied together all along, since that moment when he had shot her. Still, even here, even now, something like a magical bond linked them.

She had never contemplated what an intimate act murder might be: to feel with a shock of pain and invasion his knife tear into her belly. She put her hand down and felt the warm blood thawing its numbness. To have this man of all men thrusting into her . . . And, in a burst of light as fierce as any she had yet experienced, she understood finally, clearly, why she had been sent back; what it was that only she could do. Not to trap him, not to kill him, not even to imprison him. It was this moment, and she, and she alone, who could set him free. And herself as well, by doing so.

The snow became a vortex into which she was falling, falling, down, down, down . . . She must say it before she vanished: 'I forgive you,' she whispered.

This time, it was true.

* * *

She sagged in his arms, eyes closing, lips parting on a final breath.

Christ, he had killed her. His head swam. What if she really had been . . . ? She'd said something as she died — what? *I forgive you.* That was it; that was what she'd said. Something surged through him, like an electric current.

In a distance, as if miles away, he heard car doors slamming, someone shouting. He looked up, and there was a frizzy-haired woman with a gun — some kind of cop — and two guys, the boyfriend and another one he didn't recognize.

He'd killed her. *Jesus, Paterson, you are crazy.* He let her fall, dropped the knife with her, reached to his waistband for the empty gun, and held it out in front of him, aiming it at the redhead.

Suddenly, Catherine was out of the way, sinking to the ground in a river of red, and Paterson was in the clear. 'Catherine!' Jack yelled and ran toward her.

Behind her, Chang heard Conners hit the ground on the run. She steadied the Glock, sighted carefully — best shot in her class at the Bureau — and fired. A crimson stain blossomed like a rose in the middle of Paterson's forehead and he dropped to one knee. The gun slipped from his fingers and he collapsed in a heap in the bloody snow, one arm falling across Catherine as if to comfort her.

★ ★ ★

She was there, in the light again, just as before. She sensed familiar spirits waiting for her somewhere ahead; felt herself weightless, free of pain and care, flying into the light.

And again, someone separated herself from the whiteness and moved toward her. Catherine squinted, and felt her heart turn over.

'Mommy!' a voice that seemed to be within her cried.

'Becky?' she asked, thrilled beyond all meaning. 'Becky, is it really you?' She remembered then what Gabronski had said about her guardian spirit: without sex, without age. And knew who had been guiding her all along.

They embraced. Even without a physical self, she could sense the arms encircling her; knew that she held her daughter to her breast once again; knew that her tears flowed.

'My darling, I'll never let you go again,' Catherine vowed. 'We will be together forever.'

After a moment, Becky seemed to retreat from her slightly. 'No, you must go back.'

'No, no, I can't. I won't!' Catherine cried and reached out, trying to grab her daughter back to her, but Becky was receding. 'Don't leave me, Becky. Don't go.'

'You must go back.' Her voice was growing fainter. 'You must take care of my baby sister. But I will be with you always. My love will never leave you, nor yours me.'

'Becky,' Catherine sobbed again. The silvery glow was swirling, eddying about her. A drop of light, turned liquid, fell upon her cheek. She opened her eyes, and found herself lying in the snow, in Jack's arms.

Beyond him, from a far, far distance, someone shouted, 'They're on their way!'

'Catherine, hold on,' Jack sobbed, kissing her brow. 'Don't leave me again, darling. I couldn't bear it.'

Her lips parted, and she found the breath to whisper faintly, 'I'm here.' She closed her eyes, and felt another of his tears fall upon her cheek.

THE END

We do hope that you have enjoyed reading this large print book.

Did you know that all of our titles are available for purchase?

We publish a wide range of high quality large print books including:
Romances, Mysteries, Classics
General Fiction
Non Fiction and Westerns

Special interest titles available in large print are:
The Little Oxford Dictionary
Music Book, Song Book
Hymn Book, Service Book

Also available from us courtesy of Oxford University Press:
Young Readers' Dictionary
(large print edition)
Young Readers' Thesaurus
(large print edition)

For further information or a free brochure, please contact us at:
Ulverscroft Large Print Books Ltd.,
The Green, Bradgate Road, Anstey,
Leicester, LE7 7FU, England.
Tel: (00 44) **0116 236 4325**
Fax: (00 44) **0116 234 0205**

Other titles in the
Linford Mystery Library:

THE DARK CORNERS & OTHER STORIES

Robert J. Tilley

A schoolboy disappears — but the missing child may not be all he seemed . . . A mortician and his family find their new neighbours disturbingly interested in their affairs . . . Quiet Mr. Wooller finds himself the only man ready to take down the Devil . . . An escaped convict stumbles upon an apparently idyllic holiday cottage . . . A spouses' golf game ends in murder . . . In an outwardly perfect marriage, one partner is making dark dealings . . . A young man is subjected to a bizarre hostage-taking . . . Seven unsettling stories from the pen of Robert J. Tilley.

THE SYMBOL SEEKERS

A. A. Glynn

In 1867 a box treasured by a distin-
guished American exile in England is
stolen. Three battle-hardened ex-Southern
soldiers from the recently ended American Civil War arrive on an unusual
mission: two go on a hectic pursuit of
the box in Liverpool and London, whilst
third takes a path that could lead to
the gallows. Detective Septimus Dacers
and Roberta Van Trask, the daughter
of an American diplomat, risk their
lives as they attempt to foil a grotesque
scheme that could cause war between
Britain and the United States . . .

SONS OF THE SPHINX

Norman Firth

'We have read of your intended expedition to Egypt, to the Pyramid of Khufu . . . Only death can be your lot if you embark upon this journey. The Sons of the Sphinx.' So reads the sinister message in fine Arabic script mailed to a Hollywood movie producer. But the filming goes ahead — and the body of his chief cameraman is found with his throat cut . . . While in *Corpses Don't Care*, the grand opening of a luxury hotel is ruined by a series of six corpses turning up in the most inconvenient places!

THE LION'S GATE

V. J. Banis

On holiday with her wayward sister Allison at a lakeside town, Peggy Conners is perplexed when Allison packs her bags and vanishes overnight, without explanation. Believing her sister to be in great danger, Peggy eventually traces and confronts her, now living on an island at the Lions family mansion. But then Allison asserts that her name is actually Melissa Lions — and that she has never seen Peggy before in her life!

HOLLYWOOD HEAT

Arlette Lees

1950s Los Angeles: When six-year-old Daisy Adler vanishes from her upscale Hollywood Hills home, Detective Rusty Hallinan enters a case with more dangerous twists and turns than Mulholland Drive. Hallinan's life hits a bump or two of its own when he's dumped by his wife and falls for an enchanting young murder suspect half his age. But what's the connection between her murdered husband and a dying bar-room stripper? How does Hallinan's informant, exotic and endangered female impersonator Tyrisse Covington, fit into the puzzle? And where has little Daisy gone?